I0609898

BECOMING

MATTHEW LEDREW

BECOMING

CORAL BEACH CASEFILES

Published in Canada by Engen Books, St. John's, NL.

A CIP catalogue record for this book is available from Library and Archives Canada.

ISBN: 978-1-989473-15-3
Copyright © 2019 Matthew LeDrew

NO PART OF THIS BOOK MAY BE REPRODUCED OR TRANSMITTED IN ANY FORM OR BY ANY MEANS, ELECTRONIC OR MECHANICAL, INCLUDING PHOTOCOPYING AND RECORDING, OR BY ANY INFORMATION STORAGE OR RETRIEVAL SYSTEM WITHOUT WRITTEN PERMISSION FROM THE AUTHOR, EXCEPT FOR BRIEF PASSAGES QUOTED IN A REVIEW.

This book is a work of fiction. Names, characters, places and incidents are products of the author's imagination or are used fictitiously. Any resemblance to actual events or locales or persons living or dead is entirely coincidental.

Distributed by:
Engen Books
www.engenbooks.com
submissions@engenbooks.com

First mass market paperback printing: April 2011
Second mass market paperback printing: August 2019

Cover Image: Kit Sora Photography

KIT SORA PHOTOGRAPHY

For
Ellen

PREVIOUSLY IN
BLACK WOMB

Life is hard when you're a teenager.

That's even truer in the rural town of Coral Beach, Maine.

In the past four months, the little town has quickly become the murder capital per capita of the United States. Besieged by gang violence for years, things escalated with the sudden death of Jamie Dawkins, a local celebrity football player, near the start of the school year. Both police and the local gang, the Tees, blamed the event on a rival gang called the Omegas from the next town over, Coral Cove. This resulted in the tenuous peace between the two territories to unravel, followed quickly by full-scale assaults and retaliation from both sides.

But Jamie's death wasn't the fault of either gang, which soon became apparent when more and more bodies started to pile up. The truth was something far more sinister: there was a serial killer in Coral Beach.

Suspicion fell on Alexander 'Xander' Drew, a local teen who was known among his classmates for fitting the loner profile of so many schoolyard mass murderers that had come before him: lonely, bookish, and dangerously introverted. Although evidence persisted, there were some who refused to believe that Xander could be a killer, including Sara Johnson, his long-time friend and unrequited love.

The truth was stranger than anyone could have imagined at the time: Xander had been born Adam Evensong, and was a part of a long line of fetal experiments conducted by a mysterious organization known only as Engen. He'd been deemed a failure and was slated to be terminated, but was saved by his estranged mother and placed into foster care.

At the age of sixteen, Xander's latent abilities that Engen had thought they'd failed to instill started to manifest, creating a separate consciousness that lay dormant inside him until it broke free, turning him into a blackened monstrosity of teeth and talons and fear: the Black Womb.

With the help of their agent Adam Genblade, Engen manipulated events in Coral Beach to feed into the Womb's bloodlust and train it how to be a killer. The domino effect set a vicious series of events in motion. A conspiracy so elaborate that it not only resulted in the birth of the Black Womb, but also in the corruption of Derek Smith into the serial killer that had taken Jamie's life and culminating in the death of Xander's best friend and confidant, Sara Johnson.

In the months following, Xander has made good on a promise made at her funeral to stop the innocent people of his town from falling victim to Engen and their machinations. After weeks of effort, he has successfully beaten back the Tee gang, put Adam Genblade in a coma that his doctors say he'll never wake up from, and finally started to move on from the loss of Sara by dating Julie Peterson.

Recently his control over his alter ego has improved dramatically, and he has been slowly learning to control his radical temper with the help of school guidance counselor and psychologist Dr. Warren O'Toole.

Despite that, a recent hunt to find a missing child has put his relationship with Julie on the rocks. Although he eventually chose his personal life over his professional one, their status as a couple remains unclear...

BECOMING
CHAPTER ONE

He felt cold.

Unnaturally cold, the type of chill that starts from your heart and pumps its way through your entire body. Cold that freezes you slowly, starting with your blood, then moves to your muscle tendons, your flesh, and your hair. Your eyes are the last to go, still skittering about in their sockets, watching all of the paralyzed parts of you that your brain orders to move fail to do so until you're a living statue of ice.

All around him was dark and black and death; everything was filled with that death. That weight that pulls you down into the shadows and won't let go until it has you forever. Where you can't even see the knife in your own hand before you stab yourself just so you can stop feeling the cold.

He felt his arm twitch, but without the benefit of seeing he wondered if it had only been his imagination. The only thing he knew for certain was that there was blood somewhere. He could smell it. After all this time being absorbed in it, drowned in it, its scent had become more familiar than any he had ever known. That red coppery tang was more familiar to him than the smell of an oven-baked apple pie to most.

It was home.

He ran his hands over himself, rummaging about in the darkness to make sure the red fluid was not coming from him and that he wasn't dying. His touch was freezing and not his own, as though he were poking at himself with thick gloves.

Somewhere there was a steady hissing noise, but it was faint enough to ignore for now. He blocked it out and continued to pat down his flesh to see if it was wet with redness and death. There was none, but he now realized that he was naked. Naked and cold in the dark, black room, with nothing but soft, mechanical hissing to keep him company.

"Ugh."

His head shot up, making his hair bounce and several strands fall into his eyes. He stared into the darkness, waiting for the sound to happen again, not sure if he was looking in the right direction or if his nose was two feet from a solid wall.

"Ah."

He heard it again. A moan, but not of pleasure. It was agonized, filled with pain. It sounded almost moist, if sounds were capable of such texture, as though the person speaking were drowning. He noticed that each syllable was accompanied by a clicking noise, the long scrape of metal against metal.

There was harsh, labored breathing now, both from him and whomever was out there in the darkness calling out in pain. It was definitely coming from the direction he was facing now. There was no wall, he was sure of it.

"...help..."

She was small and tender, and he recognized her somehow. He recognized her cry for aid as if he'd heard it a thousand times before.

He tried to get up but found that he couldn't, the fatty tissue of his calf sticking to the freezing cold floor. There was a deep, sick tearing sound that got worse each time he tried, but he felt no pain and kept rocking back and forth until he was free, leaving behind a tattered maw of flesh.

He held his hands under his armpits to try and keep them from freezing and stumbled forward, almost falling after the first step but somehow pressing on. His teeth chattered. He felt the urge to urinate come to him then leave again at a rapid pace as the chill reached his bladder. He tried to call out to find out where the voice was coming from, but he could not.

"...please..."

It came again, and he felt a deep pang within his chest, in a place that he had gone to great lengths to hide from a cruel world that had beaten and tortured his very soul into submission. It was his heart, he realized, as grim determination set in to counteract the cold. The pangs he felt were a lover's pain, the longing to help and to be helped, to love and to be loved. His heart wanted to find this girl and preserve the feeling she brought as long as possible.

He tripped and fell to the ground which had been so soft before and now was as hard and unforgiving as stone. His knees scraped its ragged surface, rending flesh and drawing out blood. He gritted his teeth to howl as something penetrated his knee cap, but again, no sound would come. His voice was afraid to be heard in the darkness, he wondered why.

Something moved in the dark.

He turned toward it, terrorized sweat running down his brow as he squinted, trying to find the source of the motion. But still, all he could see was the black. The black that seemed to both go on forever and to end right in front of his face. Something slithered there just beyond his senses, snaking about in the dark, brought forth by the smell of the blood that was already freezing to his skin.

With a grunt he forced himself to his feet again, limping his way into the hollow that stretched out before him.

"...love..."

Love? Was that why he kept going, refusing to lay down and die? To stop the madness that had enveloped his darkness, threatening to swallow him whole? Somewhere inside he screamed yes and wanted to be heard. He wanted to tell her that he was here, that he was coming, that she need not fear. And yet he did not, for fear itself had its plump fingers wrapped around his neck.

"Ah."

He stopped. The voice no longer came from in front of him. He looked around, searching it out, trying in vain to regain his bearings when there had been none to begin with. His lip quivered as he searched, his teeth clenching to stop the chatter until his gums bled from pressure and point.

Something skittered before him, coming from above and below. Left and right. It was everywhere. It was as if the darkness itself was what was attacking him, frightening him, keeping him from the person that he wanted so desperately to help. The skittering stopped for a moment, as if the thing had only just noticed him. He got the distinct impression that he was being watched, like great eyes were upon him. He felt like now that he was in their sights, they would never let go. Like his life would be spent forever running away.

A new cool came over him, far more bitter than the last. It was the chill of fear: that harsh, tingly numbness that comes with being stalked, being observed, being forlorn.

"...please..."

He turned around completely, too shocked and frustrated by the new direction of the sound to care about the attacker now. It wasn't about him; the only thing that mattered was her.

Her.

She lay in the center of a pale stream of light that had not been there before, and he wondered how he had missed it. Her body was sprawled out like a star. She lay there, unmoving, unwavering. Her long raven hair was all around her, drawn in a misshapen circle with the pale skin of her cheeks and the whites of her eyes in its center. Her lips were as red as the very mouth of the fire burning brightly in the dark and igniting flames within him as he limped forward. Her eyes were as dark and hollow as the air that surrounded him, but he felt as though he could look into them forever without dread or regret. Life would not pass him by looking into those eyes, for his life was contained within them. Her breast rose and fell peacefully, if rapidly, and her slender neck and collar moved in unison, throbbing each time she swallowed. She was draped in a red cloth that did little to cover her slender, smooth white legs, she looked like an angel wrapped in the clothes of the devil.

She was beautiful.

"Eve?" he whispered, so low that she could barely hear. She turned toward him as he knelt next to her, reaching for her hand and clasping it tightly inside both of his.

A smile spread over his lips as their fingers met and he could no longer feel the cold.

"Adam..." she gasped, though she was not surprised. Her every breath was labored. It was as if she had to fight to find her voice, and he had to fight to hear it. Her eyes welled up, tears beginning to flow from their corners. "You came."

"Of course," Adam said gently, caressing the side of her face as he bent down and kissed her hand, softly. He ran a finger through her hair, and it was as smooth and silky as it looked.

"I'm sorry..." she said sadly, her lower lip trembling. "I'm sorry I had to go."

Her voice whined at the end involuntarily, the unshed tears in her throat distorting her voice.

"You don't have to go anywhere," he hushed her and kissed her forehead desperately. The salt water dribbling down his cheeks made a liar of him. He raised his hand to run it through his hair, then stopped, and looked at it. The fingers were stained with red, so red that it was almost black. When he looked back at her, he saw that the red cloth was not as long as he had thought. He saw that it was not cloth that covered at all: it was red liquid that seeped into the patch of light surrounding her.

"Honey, I have to," she sobbed, staring into his soul and shattering it forevermore.

"Then I'll come with you." he gasped, bending over her body as the sobs raked through him, making his body quiver and shake. "I can, I will... I'll come with you..."

"No, baby..." she chided, using all the energy she had to bring a finger to his lip, calming him. "No, you have to stay. You can't follow me where I'm going, honey. You mustn't."

"Please, please..." he sobbed, tears seemingly coming from his nose and mouth as well as his eyes now, coming from any place they could, just needing to get out. "Please, don't leave me. Don't leave me here all alone, please...I'll do anything. I'll be better, I will. I promise I will. Please...just please, don't leave me..."

His body shook and convulsed as hers stopped. He paused after a moment and realized that he was talking to himself, and that she was gone. Still crying, he leaned in slowly, kissing her lightly on the lips and then turning away, unable to watch as his heart of hearts broke.

When he opened his eyes again, a second stream of light had appeared, spotlighting someone new.

"Adam," *the deep, scratchy voice bellowed, as it stood proud in the spotlight, its back arched. It was made of the darkness, tiny scales of shadow linked together to make a form that only vaguely resembled human. It was sleek and smooth, its skin almost like that of a seal's, oily in its purity. Its red eyes were slanted triangles, the tips pointing into curves, forming half-spirals. It was muscular, but not overly so. Lean. At the tip of each long, slender finger was a talon about four inches in length, gleaming in the pale light. It growled at all times, even when it spoke.*

"Black Womb," Adam sneered, standing up. He no longer cared that he was naked in the dark, that he was cold, or that he was afraid. All that mattered was the red smear on his hand, and the despicable creature which had caused it.

"Black Womb lives!" *it yelled, leaping forward at Adam. It crossed the distance between them in two great bounds. When it sprang it did so claws first, plunging their serrated edges deep into Adam's chest.*

"Argh!" Adam cried, lashing out with his sword and digging it deep into the Womb's shoulder.

Had there been a sword before?

The creature grabbed Adam by both shoulders and pulled him forward, forcing the blade deeper into its own flesh. Smiling a wicked, toothy grin, it brought both feet up and dug its toe-talons into Adam's chest, locking the naked man in. It bent over quickly as if to touch its toes, lashing out into Adam's face with its claws.

"She made me!" *it yelled frantically, pleading even as it ravaged Adam's cheeks and lips savagely.* "I had no choice! She made it for me, don't you get that, you murdering freak?"

"So, I'm the freak?" *Adam sneered, grabbing it by the neck and pushing so hard its back slammed into the floor. The sword scraped into the metal tiling, effectively stapling the Womb to it.* "Take a look in the mirror lately?"

"Rahh!" *the Womb roared, pushing out with his legs and flipping Adam over onto his stomach. It reached up and pulled the blood-soaked sword from its central plexus as if it were nothing. It stood up and spun the blade between its fingers.* "You think it's so tragic, what happened to Eve, but what about what happened to me? What about what you did to me?"

The Womb plunged the sword down through Adam's back, severing his spinal cord and pinning him there with his face pressed against the floor. Sneering, the creature drew back a foot and kicked Adam in the head again and again, sending blood and saliva squirting into the darkness in V-shaped spurts.

The Womb stopped as Adam struggled for breath, forcing himself to look up at his attacker. The creature sneered.

"Look at what you're making me do now," *it chuckled, before raising its foot high once more...*

ʎ✕ʎ

Xander woke with a start, his nose freezing.

He tried hard to open his eyes, finding that it was almost impossible. It was like they had been sealed shut, and when he did finally manage to open them, it was accompanied by a tearing sound. He wiped them with the backs of his hands, discovering that they'd been covered in a hard yellow crust so thick that it came off in one great layer.

"Gah," he gasped, taking a deep breath as sweat dribbled down his face and chin. The salty putrid stench of perspiration was all he could smell. His underarms were bathed in it. It stung at the cracks in his lips and made his irises sore. His hair, damp with it, clung to his head.

Everything around him was white, even his hands. Smooth, silky white covered everything that he was. As his eyes adjusted and his vision came into focus, he discovered that his hands were actually a disturbing purple colour, with veins popping out their backs. His entire form was shivering now, quaking like a leaf on the wind as fresh mucus clung to his nose like tiny icicles while freezing his mouth shut.

He raised his hands slowly. It took considerable effort. They were numb beyond the telling of the word and it felt as though he were carrying weights attached to each finger. His palms were red, every pore in them open, full and tinged with tiny black flecks. He could look into them as if they were black holes. He put his hands back down into the white, silky cold that surrounded him and scooped it up into a tiny ball, mashing it with his right hand.

It was snow.

He tilted his head up to watch it fall. Thousands of snowflakes glittered in the air, each one different from the next, or so people said. Each one traveled gently, carefully down until finally resting with the others, settling in as if it belonged there. Undisturbed, snow was nature at its very best.

The flakes fell between the trees, some of them sticking

to hefty branches and weighing them down, making them look sad and droopy. The trees hung above him, leaning in as if to surround him, leaving him no alternative but to stay in his little clearing, freezing and naked.

It's night, he realized. It was the first thought his addled brain produced. He still didn't quite know why that was so important. With all of his senses screaming how cold it was at once, all wanting a warm bath and a smoke at once, it was nearly impossible to think. There was a hard throb an inch above his right eye that was pounding at him, and he felt like that part of his brain was actually trying to escape.

For an instant, he was confronted with the horrible mental picture that his brain was actually a baby that was kicking the inside of his skull the way a normal child would kick at the inside of its mother's womb.

He got a flash of the child breaking free finally, its chubby fat leg pushing out through his forehead, sending brain matter and bits of bone spewing down into the white of the snow.

"Guh."

He tried to concentrate, but he had what could only have been described as brain freeze on mushrooms, slowing his thoughts down to a crawl.

Closing his eyes and willing himself to move, he stood up. He clenched and unclenched his fists a few times to try and get the blood circulating to them again, then moved his legs and wriggled his toes to make sure he still could. He could not feel them, and had to bend over to see if they were moving.

The Womb never wakes me up at night.

The thought came to him from nowhere, and it came from a voice that was not his own. He'd read stories about people able to pick up transmissions before... radio stations on high-end frequencies being heard by war vets with plates in their heads. Glasses that picked up the signal from baby-monitors when filled to just the right depth. Teeth fillings that made an electric hum when brought too close to a microphone. He'd always thought they were bullshit, but sometimes the thoughts in his head were so strange to him that he couldn't help but remember tabloid headlines like: *My son gets broadcasts from Outer Space!*

He squinted as he looked around, scanning between the trees for any sign of movement. There was a squirrel perched on a branch ten feet away, looking at Xander and the snow with equal amazement.

"Hello, Bob," Xander chuckled.

Satisfied that he was alone, he began to examine himself.

There was no blood on him.

In the past four months, Xander had learned a small set of rules for dealing with situations like this. There were things that happened when he was taken over by his Mr. Hyde persona and things that did not. One was the eye colour. It was an odd physical marker that went along with the personality shifts and one that he hadn't been able to explain yet, but whenever he was the consciousness in charge of his other form he had stark red eyes. Whenever the Womb was in control, it had putrid green eyes.

Another thing was the blood.

Whenever the Womb left him and the second skin fell

away like a snake's, there was a thin layer of blood left behind. He'd come to understand it to some degree: that it acted in much the same way a normal person's blood-brain barrier worked. It was supposed to separate them, to protect them from things the immune system simply wasn't equipped to handle.

It was a disgusting and awkward treat that was left behind whenever the Womb was forced back inside. If it wasn't present now, then the Womb hadn't retreated under normal circumstances.

"It wanted to bring me here," Xander deduced, looking around with new eyes, searching for some reason that his other half would be so specific as to bring him here on the first snow of winter.

The trees all had faces, great massive noses and sagging mouths that gaped, looking ravenous and insatiable. The moonlight bounced off of the virgin snow and reflected it in all directions, creating eerie illumination that made the faces move to speak or to eat, their great jaws chomping away at the winter night like ravenous wolves hungering for their prey.

"Look at what you're making me do now..."

Xander shuddered at the memory.

Something brushed past him, sharp against his shoulder blade. The hairs on his back stood on end and he turned around quickly, his fists clenched before him like a boxer's.

There was nothing there, and the feeling of cold, boney fingers gripping his shoulders was still upon him, digging in even deeper now.

When he looked west he could see lights. He knew

then that he was no more than a few yards from his house, and even closer to where Sara used to live. He sighed deeply, bending down again to get a better look through the branches and into town. He placed his hand down in the snow for leverage, then immediately yanked it back and gasped.

Blood poured from a long slice going down his palm, dripping into the cold snow and staining it red. He looked into the snow where it had been, but there was nothing there. Nothing sharp enough that it would cut him, except for the snow. Everything was colder here, harder, sharper than it was any other day. Even the snow could slice you open, rip you inside out. Feed on you. He'd felt this way before, just not in real life. Not in a place that he knew so well, where he had climbed trees and caught apples and gotten stung by bees.

This was death.

Cold, hard and sharp. He was sure of it now, as sure as he had ever been of anything. No more than twenty feet out the back door of his house, and he was in the presence of death.

The fingers on his shoulders gripped him harder.

He began to walk toward home.

BECOMING
CHAPTER TWO

-BEEP-

-BEEP-

-BEEP-

"Did you check the pan?"

"I am right now, checking the pan."

"Good, because I really didn't want to have to have that fight with you again."

"Would you shut up?"

"I'm just saying..."

"You keep throwing that back in my face. One time I didn't check the pan. One time."

"Hey, I just don't want to come in tomorrow and find a big - "

"One! Time!"

"All right, all right. Sheesh, just check it already, and stop talking about it."

"I told you, I'm checking the pan."

"And?"

"And as sick as this guy was when he was awake, the

stuff I find in the pan brings new meaning to the word."

"That's why you check the pan, and I check the heart monitor."

"How is he today, anyway?"

- -

"How is his heart rate?"

- -

"Hello? Crazy lady? I asked you a question. What is his heart rate like today?"

"Hmm? Oh... it's spiking. Every few minutes."

"Spiking?"

"Yeah... looks like little Adam Genblade is having nightmares."

"Huh."

"I wonder what it takes to scare a sick fuck like him anyway."

ﾉﾍﾉ

She giggled, her nose crinkling just a little as she did, in the cutest possible way. Just like the way that she did everything else, it was all just about as wonderfully peaceful as it could be.

The sun was shining. It was a beautiful summer day, and there were warm rays against their backs.

The picnic basket lay neatly on the red and white checkered tablecloth, spread out against the greenest grass God ever put on this earth. Ants crawled around the plates, their feelers twitching at the scent of apple pie and boxes of cranberry juice.

"More strawberries?" Adam asked, quickly reaching up a hand to make sure that his hair was all right. It was, perfectly molded and quaffed by half a pound of extra-hold gel. He had wanted it to look perfect for her, but now he worried that it

looked like a dirty blond hard hat sitting on his scalp.

Eve giggled at him again, a bubbly sound, like fresh water from a spring well.

"I saw that," she taunted, scolding him playfully by waving a finger at him. "What are you all dressed up for today, anyway?"

"Oh, I don't know," he smiled, leaning a little closer to her. His nostrils flared to pick up more of the divine perfume she was wearing. He could not pin down what it smelled like, but he knew that it was good. "I guess I just felt the need to be half as pretty as you are for a change."

"Aww," she cooed, tapping him playfully on the face. "You're so sweet."

He winked at her.

She rolled her eyes, then took one of the strawberries from the bowl near him and put it past her pearly white teeth and her soft, red lips. She bit down, sucking on what remained.

He felt the hairs on the back of his neck stand on end. It always amazed him how she could be so sensual in everyday things... in everything she did, really. How she could turn him on with just a look, or the way that her raven hair fell across her breasts a certain way... or the way she could say his name when he wasn't feeling good and make all of the bad things in his life melt away.

The wind picked up and the trees all around them swayed with the breeze.

"How was the casserole?" he asked, looking down as he played with the last bit of mashed potato on his plate with the end of his plastic knife.

"It was great, baby," she assured him, motioning toward her empty plate as proof. She ate whatever he cooked anyway, even if *it tasted like garbage, as it almost always did. "I loved it."*

She smiled, plucking the stem off a strawberry before holding the rest out to him.

He leaned in and took it into his mouth, keeping his eyes on hers the entire time, watching them light up as he kissed her fingers before he started chewing the strawberry.

"These are really fresh," she commented, picking up another and plucking the stem off of it, running the pointed side along her lips before putting it in her mouth. "Where did you get them, the deli?"

"Picked them myself. I put a few of them in the fruit salad, too..."

"I noticed. It made it sweeter. Probably your best yet, hun."

Adam looked down, his cheeks turning a little red.

"No need to blush, lover," she cooed, reaching out and tilting his chin up. "This was perfect. It was just what I needed."

He smiled, blushing even more now that he knew that she had noticed it. "I know that work's been tough on you lately..."

"Work has been a nightmare." she giggled, lying back on the tablecloth. "Anderson pulled some strings and got his cousin out of the mail room (where he belongs) and up into the editing suite. I swear, there were at least fifty mistakes in last night's run, and who gets fired? Lorraine, that's who."

"He really fired Lorraine?"

"Yeah."

"That's awful."

"So, his little knob cousin gets her position, and..."

"Wait, he messes up, someone else gets fired, and he gets a promotion?"

"Uh-huh."

"*That's insane.*"

"*That's television, babe.*"

"*I honestly don't know how you can handle working with those vultures. I would've fed Anderson through the tape deck long ago.*"

"*It's simple,*" she said slyly, crawling over the plates to get closer to him. "*I've got you to come home to, big guy.*"

He grinned as she leaned in to kiss him, making no motion forward as she did. Their lips met, and the sweet taste of strawberries rubbed off onto his tongue as her own came into his mouth, hot and fast, making his body tingle all over.

Suddenly her eyes shot open and her nails dug into his side.

He opened his eyes and looked at her, seeing her panic and fear. Their lips parted, but hers still moved, trying to tell him something, trying to let him know. He drew back the hand that had been wrapped around her waist, and found that it was covered in blood. Silky, red blood that dribbled down his arm to his rolled up sleeves. It soaked into the shirt he'd taken so long to pick out and expanded, soaking ever outward until it was drenched in her.

Her body slumped against the tablecloth, staining the white checkers red until the cloth wasn't checkered at all anymore. It was just red. Her face landed in what was left of his mashed potatoes.

He wondered if she had even liked the potatoes, really.

He looked up.

A young man stood just on the edge of the cloth, dressed completely in black. A cigarette hung loosely between his lips as he took small puffs, blowing them out through his nose. In his hand was a small blood-stained dagger with a handle that was *etched into the shape of a dragon. He couldn't have been any older than sixteen, but his face was worn and scarred, the face of a young man who had seen too many fights in his life. His jaw was steadfast and unwavering despite the horrible thing he had just done. His eyes were black, covering his entire eye like one great pupil.*

"What have you done?" Adam screamed, looking from his fallen lover to the madman that stood before him, cold and uncaring. There must have been some mistake. She was everything to him, all that he lived for. Rolling over and seeing her was his sole reason for opening his eyes every morning, and knowing that he could do it again the next day was his reason for closing them at night. She was his rock. His peace. His everything.

"Why would you do this to her?" he sobbed, tears streaming down his face. "What could she have possibly done?"

The boy snarled, spitting the burning cigarette out of his mouth. It landed in Eve's hair and singed it, filling the air with the rank stench of burning hair and starch. He raised his blade and brought it down swiftly, slicing down Adam's cheek and drawing blood.

Adam stumbled backward onto the tablecloth. He felt it soak into his arms and lower back as though it wasn't even a cloth at all anymore... it was a shallow pool of Eve's blood, somehow suspended in a perfect square in the center of the grassy knoll. He threw his free arm back to try and catch himself, but only succeeded in twisting his wrist in. Pain shot through his arm as he stared at the boy, who met his gaze head on as he opened his mouth to speak.

"Black Womb sends his regards."

Adam's eyes went wide as the killer took one threatening step forward, twirling the blade between his fingers. For the first time, his stony face showed an emotion... and it could only be described as utter glee. He'd seen it on Eve's face a thousand times, and never would again.

"Why are you doing this?!" Adam screamed.

The killer said nothing, just took another calm step forward, followed by another.

Adam turned, scrambling to his feet and taking off toward the park. There would be someone there who could help him. Policemen patrolled the park all the time on bikes, and they'd help him.

He ran as fast as his feet would carry him. The trees around began to blur together until all he saw was a deep green tunnel curving up on either side of him as he ran. His heart slammed in his chest and he felt like he was going on forever, pounding mercilessly through the endless cave of evergreen.

He stepped on the shards of a broken beer bottle, and only then realized that he hadn't been wearing shoes. He'd taken them off sometime while he was eating his fruit salad.

Pain erupted through his leg and he fell, tumbling end over end down an embankment he hadn't seen a moment ago.

There were rocks pressed into his face. Mud and pine needles stuck all through his hair and made him look wild, like a man of the forest itself. He tasted blood in the back of his throat and wasn't sure if it was his own or not. His breath was so heavy that it stung at his chest. Everything hurt. The skin of his cheek had been ripped off by an errant branch at some point during the fall.

The boy stood at the top of the hill, only a shadowy black outline visible against the clear spring sky.

Adam stared at him, unable to do anything but take those heavy, labored breaths. He could not take his eyes off of him.

A wry, toothy grin spread over the boy's face, starkly white against his black silhouette. He hopped down onto the incline of dirt and moss and began to skid his way down the embankment.

Adam cursed, pushing himself up off the ground and running again. There was glass sticking out of his foot and a rock caught between one eye and its lid, but he kept running. Eve would want him to keep running.

The grass that had felt so nice before now sunk beneath his heavy feet as he tried desperately to get away, to be anywhere but here. He left small pools of dark red behind him in each footprint, the glass working its way in and out with every impact.

The killer walked calmly, one foot in front of the other, still twirling the blade as he went. He juggled it between his hands like some deranged circus clown, complete with a painted grin. He wasn't running, or even walking fast, but somehow he was still gaining on Adam. It was like Adam was running in place.

Adam turned to face forward, seeing nothing but the haze of trees and moss again.

Hadn't there been a path here?

Sweat poured down his brow as he realized that he had made a wrong turn somewhere, that he wasn't heading for the police or the park or anything else. Glancing around quickly, he grabbed up a large stick, pulled it free of its branch, and tried his best to look menacing through his blinding fear.

He turned around.

Nothing.

No killer, no knives, and no dead lover. Just evergreens and furs and a scant few maples looking back at him, their trunks like long faces, ready to devour him at a moment's notice.

It was suddenly very cold.

The sun was gone now, hidden behind some rather ominous looking clouds that had come out of nowhere. Twigs from the branch cut into his palms, but he dared not let it go. He smacked his lips together, trying to bring some moisture to their stale, arid surface. They still tasted like strawberries.

"Oh, god..." he cried softly, tears welling up in his eyes. "Oh, god no..."

"Don't bother asking God for help," came a voice from behind him.

He turned quickly, only to find himself face to face with the killer.

"You'll be seeing him soon enough."

Adam's lower lip quivered as he raised his stick high.

The killer lashed out with the blade, driving it into the branch Adam was holding. It dissected it easily, the blade pierced it right to the hilt.

Adam yelped.

The boy twisted then pulled back hard, breaking the branch apart and turning it to splinters within Adam's grasp. Some drove into his palm and he screamed. It was almost as bad as the glass had been, the sticky sap stinging at the wound and making his flesh swell and pound.

"Why are you doing this?" Adam wailed. "Why would you hurt her?"

"She made me do it, Adam," the killer snarled, becoming visibly enraged by the question. "She made me kill her. You and her, you made me. You made the Black Womb."

"I don't know anything about any Black Womb, I swear," Adam pleaded. "Just tell him that he's got the wrong people, I'm sure he'll understand..."

"Why don't you tell him yourself?!" the killer screamed, as

his skin began to turn a charred black. It came from him like a tidal wave, a giant mouth crashing down onto Adam with thousands of tiny teeth ripping into his flesh, sucking the marrow from his bones and the blood from his veins.

It swirled and spun around him, ripping at his flesh and tearing at him, as though he were caught in the center of a tornado made of knives. He tried to scream but couldn't, his voice lost in the maelstrom.

The wave of blackness crashed upon the trees and crashed back onto itself, filling the space the killer had occupied until he was whole and solid once again.

All that was left to Adam was a pile of bones too thick to be devoured.

Calmly, the killer reached into his pocket, drew out a smoke, lit it, and took a deep drag.

After holding his breath for several, long moments, he blew out a trail of smoke from each nostril.

He smirked, looked down at the bones, then chuckled to himself a little. "Black Womb lives."

⋏⋏

Genblade's heart raced, his body convulsing inside of the restraints that kept him pinned to his hospital bed, thrusting uncontrollably.

"Nurse Reilly!" Porter called, her hairnet flying as she bent over to pin Genblade down. "Reilly, get in here!"

Reilly ran around the corner from the adjacent room, immediately rushing to Genblade's side and helping Porter pin him down. "Press the button for the orderlies! We have to get him restrained! He'll break his own neck if he keeps this up!"

Porter turned and slammed a red button next to the bed, buzzing for reinforcements, then returned to her position atop Genblade's arm. "He needs sedatives! His heart rate is off the scale, I think he's having an attack!"

Suddenly Genblade stopped, laying lifelessly in his bed again.

Reilly pushed a strand of hair back behind her ear. "What the hell was that?"

"I dunno. Whatever it is, if it keeps up, it's going to kill him."

"Wouldn't that be a shame," Reilly growled, turning to the cabinet to prepare an injection.

BECOMING
CHAPTER THREE

"The first snow of winter brings out the kid in every-one," Cathy Kennessy observed, taking a careful sip of her hot chocolate. Her dark hair was mostly hidden behind the hood of her fluffy blue winter jacket, poking out in defiance here and there and refusing to be contained. Her face looked rounder in it, and unmistakably cute, with her button nose and chubby cheeks both beet red from the chill in the air. Tiny snowflakes dotted her eyelashes. She watched Tommy and Mike fling snowballs at each other from behind trees as she sat on a small, but sheltered, bench at the bus stop.

"Why are we waiting here again?" Xander asked, watching the steam rise up from her hot beverage intently, his mouth watering as his nostrils flared to take in every bit of the glorious scent that he could.

"We're waiting for the bus." She smiled, her eyes never leaving her playful lover as he carefully dipped a freshly made snowball into a nearby puddle and waited for it to freeze so that it would impact upon Tommy with the maximum amount of damage.

Xander rolled up his sleeve for a moment and looked at his arm, only to find that it was bare. Sighing, he reached out and gently took Cathy's arm, pulling her sleeve up to examine the time on her watch. "It's 8:45. The bus left, like, fifteen minutes ago."

"In that case, we're watching my man pummel the other man with cold balls of half-frozen liquid," she admitted, taking another sip of her drink then licking the excess foam from her warm, dark lips.

"Just as long as we're being honest about our total lack of punctuality regarding our academic obligations."

"Is using big words like that some lame attempt at a penis extension for you?" she blurted suddenly, turning from watching Mike to looking at him.

He stopped, giving her a droll look and holding it until she finally cracked a smile.

"Sorry," she chuckled, turning back to the boys. "I couldn't resist."

"Exactly how long have you been waiting to say that?"

"Ever since Laird Street. You said something about a gargantuan essay you had to write, I thought maybe you said words like 'gargantuan' to make up for something that is the very opposite of 'gargantuan.' But by that time you and Mike had moved on to a different subject, so I buried it away and figured it wouldn't be too long before I got the chance to use it again."

"You put that much thought into burning me?" he smirked, raising an eyebrow in her direction.

"Sometimes hours of planning," she nodded, taking some more of the hot liquid and glancing at him, finally noticing the hungered look he got on his face every time she brought it to her lips. Rolling her eyes, she took another small sip and then passed it to him without looking.

He smiled widely in anticipation, bringing the paper cup to his lips and letting the brown foam glop down his throat until it was almost gone.

"Thank you," he gasped as he came out of the cup for some air, then quickly downed the rest. He turned toward a nearby garbage can, jumped, and threw the cup while still in midair. He missed his target completely, the cup landing in the snow next to it and sinking down about an inch.

He stopped and stared at it for a moment, his shoulders slumping in defeat as he turned back around to where Cathy stared at him, shaking her head.

"You're hopeless," she mumbled, patting him once on the head. "Even with super-human abilities, you just can't seem to sink one free throw, can you?"

"Hey! Give me a sword and I'll make paper dolls out of a house! But that... that..." he huffed. "It was only a paper cup anyway. It has no mass. The wind took it."

Cathy stuck her finger into her mouth and held it up in the air. "What wind, exactly, would that be?"

"My body's blocking it from you now."

"Then move."

"I... don't want to?"

"You suck."

"I do. I really, really do."

"And it's the fact that you know that which redeems you."

"Really?" he smiled, looking up.

"Nah," she spat, brushing the notion away. "I just wanted to see your hopes get up. That shoulder slumping thing you do is just too cute."

Even as she said it, his shoulders were doing just that.

She turned back to her boyfriend playing in the snow, laughed a little, then waved at him with only her fingers. He waved back, giving Tommy the opportunity to pelt him with a custom-made ice ball, right in the side of the face.

"Blonds," she mumbled softly to herself as she watched Mike prepare to take his revenge.

Mike shook the chill off his face, then tucked what remained of his hair beneath his black and white toque. A grim, determined look came over him as he scooped up an armful of snow, winked at his girlfriend, then silently plotted his revenge against Tommy.

Tommy was behind a nearby bush, waiting for the angered Mike to come to him and his pile of balled-up death.

"So why aren't you over there playing with the moron twins?" Cathy asked, motioning to the large pile of snow at Xander's feet. "I'm sure you could make balls so big and heavy that the wind wouldn't take them."

"No thanks, I already got two like that. Besides, I kinda wanted to talk to you about something."

"Oh," Cathy sighed, frowning for the first time today. "I think I know what it is."

"You do?"

"Yeah, and I'm really sorry about what happened the other day. I know you're with Julie now, and I swear I never went over there with the intention of kissing you, I really didn't. And I really didn't mean for Mike to go after you like that. I know that things are okay between you and him now, but I still want you to know that all of this was my fault, and that it'll never happen again. I was just so hurt, and I thought you... I don't know what I thought, but it wasn't right either way. I love you, Xander, and I really don't want to do anything to jeopardize that, ever. I'm so mad at myself for some of the choices I've been making lately, you have no idea. It's like I'm not even--"

"Cathy," Xander interjected, raising a finger as if to poke it in the middle of her train of thought. "That's all very nice and all, but that's not what I wanted to talk about."

"Oh," she said, blushing and looking down a little. "Forget I said anything then."

He reached over and tilted her head upward, feeling the softness of her face. "And just for the record, it was my fault. If I'd made my feelings about the possibility of us clear, you never would have gotten so confused."

"But, I --"

He cut her off, raising the finger again.

She smiled, then reached up and pulled the finger down, clasping his hand tightly for only a moment. She mouthed a simple thank you, knowing full well that he would stop her if she tried to actually say it. "So, what's up then?"

"It's my relationship with Jules," he said glumly.

"I always thought it was unhealthy, the amount of time you spent in the science fiction section of the library," she scoffed with mock contempt, putting one hand on her hip and waving the other finger at him menacingly.

"Huh?"

"Jules Verne," she explained.

"Ah." He nodded, understanding. "That's lame, even for you."

"I didn't have time to prepare, and I thought a joke about your family jewels would be a little below the belt."

"Yeah, well I -"

"Jewels? Below the belt? Come on..."

He frowned, and she finally stopped.

"Sorry," she said, shuffling over on the cold, wooden bench so that he could sit next to her. "What's going on? Are you two having a fight?"

"I wish," Xander replied. "If we were having a fight, at least she'd be talking to me from time to time."

"Ew, silent treatment?"

"Like you wouldn't believe. I've never seen Julie go this long without talking... ever."

"She does have the gift of gab, there's no denying that."

"How bad is this?" Xander asked, grimacing as he did, knowing what the answer would be.

"Remember when I gave Mike the silent treatment?"

"That bad?"

"No," she said. Then she paused. "No, that would be how bad it would be with a normal girl. With a jabber-mouth like Julie Peterson... well, she's probably so mad right now that you should count your lucky stars she's not talking. What did you do, anyway?"

"Me?" he turned, almost snapping. "What makes you

think any of this is my fault?"

She gave him a look.

He sighed. "Oh, all I did was lead her to believe that I wanted a very serious, loving relationship (which she has never had, by the way). Then, when she finally comes around and decides that she does too and tells me that she loves me, I don't say it back."

"Ouch. Her first time saying it?"

"Dunno. But it was her first time meaning it, anyway."

"Double ouch. That girl's got a lot to think about."

"That's what she said!" he blurted, waving his hands excitedly. "How do women do that?"

"Oh, it's called having a brain," she retorted. "You might want to try it sometime. Idiot."

Xander buried his head between his legs and covered it up with his arms until he had almost vanished from the neck up, cursing himself internally. His bones ached from the night before, the cold still coming out of them despite the protection his body was supposed to offer him.

Mike bounded over to them cheerfully, a silly grin plastered all over his face. "Hey guys, what's up?" he said loudly, his nose red and sniffling.

"Oh, my, god." Cathy said slowly, looking his snow-covered body up and down. "How did you manage to lose that badly?" she asked, giving him a little slap on the arm.

"What are you talking about?" he retorted, a distinct chill in his voice. "I won this fight."

Xander turned to see Tommy hobbling toward them, his face full of snow and just the tiniest dribbles of blood seeping from his nose. "So you did."

Mike stared at Cathy, unable to stop smiling.

"What?" she asked finally, unable to understand what was happening.

He lunged at her with both arms spread wide, enveloping her in a hug that covered her little body with snow from head to foot.

"No!" she squealed, half laughing and half whining. "It's cold! It's cold! Stop!"

Tommy and Xander shot each other a look, then decided not to mimic their friend's behavior, instead turning to walk toward the school.

Tommy looked at his watch. "We've officially missed the free breakfast at the cafeteria."

"Mmm, stale hash browns that McDick's would have turned away. Be still my beating taste buds. I don't like the morning lunch lady anyway, she looks at me like she wants to get in my pants."

"Hey, that's my aunt!"

"It's a hard truth, Tommy. Deal with it." Xander sighed with fake empathy, patting his friend on the shoulder.

"What's a hard truth?" Mike asked breathlessly, as he and Cathy finally caught up.

"Is Tommy coming out of the closet again?" chimed Cathy, taking her place next to Mike.

"What?" Tommy interjected, eyes wide.

"Yeah, we've been talking about it a lot Tommy," Xander added, nodding.

"And we think it's pretty obvious," Cathy finished.

"Bastards," Tommy chuckled a little, sticking his hands in his pockets and looking down at the sidewalk.

"You guys are fucking bastards."

"Oh, I'm hurt," Mike grumbled.

Cathy turned to Xander, then, whose eyes kept darting from the sidewalk to the road ahead. Forward, then down. Forward, then down. She frowned, then leaned in close to Mike and whispered something to him.

He nodded, then continued to berate Tommy.

BECOMING
CHAPTER FOUR

George Walker sat in a car outside the Big Eight motel on Reservoir Boulevard. It was a rental with rust dotting the wheel wells, bought on the fly from one of those we-don't-ask-questions places out by the airstrip. It was a busted old Buick that stank of Cheesies and spermicide. The man who gave it to him had smiled with all thirty-two of his pearly white teeth when he passed over the keys. He'd been wearing a blue and pink checkered shirt and a straw hat held tight to his forehead by a purple ribbon, and looked like he's stepped right out of a Don Bluth movie, with his bowtie and deep, sunken eyes.

"The tank is full," the man had said while holding either side of his checkered coat. "The tank is full, and she'll get you wherever you need to go. I'd stake my reputation on it."

George hadn't responded to the words. Hadn't even really heard them, he just kept nodding until the man stopped talking and then he took the keys to the parking lot. He remembered the words now and thought of telling the man that they didn't increase the value of the purchase. Talk was cheap, after all.

He'd always been quick-witted in hindsight.

George was pushing fifty and had very thin hair that was still quite black and allowed him to fool himself about his age. His cheeks were chubby and shook whenever he moved. As the years wore on, George began to develop a bit of a gut that tended to hang over the waist of his jeans and pull at the buttons of his shirts. His shoulders were wide, and his arms spoke to a history of physical labour, bear hugs, and strong-arming; though, the firmness of muscle was softening with age and atrophy, leaving droopy pockets of flesh where his triceps used to be. He wasn't as fast as he used to be, nor was he as agile. All told, George considered himself still very fit for his age, even though he never had the opportunity to prove it.

His fingers strummed along the hard rubber of the unfamiliar steering wheel. He had turned off the radio almost twenty minutes ago, but the last song was still stuck in his head. "Panama, by Metallica," the DJ had said, though it was really by Van Halen.

When he reached the end of the song, he slammed his palms against the wheel so hard that it left a swelled red mark across them. He gripped the wheel and looked across the long parking lot of the motel that stretched before him. There was a door with a letter on it, and then a large bay window with the curtains closed. Then a door, with a letter on it, and a large bay window with the curtains closed. After that was a door, a letter on it. Next to that was a large bay window. It had curtains. They were closed. Doors, doors, doors, windows, windows, windows, curtains, curtains, curtains. He couldn't see its end, and it seemed like it would go on forever. They all looked the same, and he wondered which one he was supposed to be looking at.

He turned from the motel to the Jeep that was parked next to him. It was large, towering over his rented Buick like a bully. The passenger door encompassed nearly all the view out of his driver's side window. It shone in the sun like it was new, and was that greenish-gray, baby-shit green colour that all jeeps seemed to be. It had halogen lights The tires were spotless, all smooth and rubber and black on big, shimmering rims.

The jeep was already there when he'd arrived. He'd hoped to get here before it, but this might be better. At least now there would be no lying when he found out for sure. At least now he would know.

He let out a long breath and leaned his forehead against the steering wheel. Closing his eyes, he let his thoughts spread over him and tried to clear his mind, tried to clear his head. His father had always told him that he did too much thinking with his gut, and lord if he hadn't been right. Too much thinking with his gut had lost him his daughter, had gotten him in trouble with the town council, and now... this.

I don't know what I'm doing here, he thought. His hands fell away from the wheel and came to rest sadly on his lap. The sun outside beat down hard and not even the fall breeze or the air conditioner fought it well, baking his exposed forearms and coating them with sweat.

"Now I don't want to hear any of that from you," said the frail old man in the passenger seat next to him.

George turned and looked at him as though just now realizing he was there, his head never leaving the wheel as he moved it.

The man had a big red nose and wore a tweed cap slanted to one side. His smile was so big it made his ears wiggle. His eyes were pale blue, so pale they looked ghostly. His name was Richard Walker, and he was George's father. "You're here because you want to be here."

"That's not true," George whispered, shaking his head just a little. "I don't want this. I don't want any of this."

Richard snorted, then turned away from him and stared out the side window. They sat in silence for six full minutes, according to the dash clock, before he finally spoke again:

"Giant eighty-foot water slide," he said, with the firm and authoritative voice of a circus showman.

George cocked his eyebrow and turned, slowly, to look at the old man.

Richard smiled that ear-wiggle smile at him again, then turned back toward the window. "Lasik eye surgery, only $499. Well, you can keep it."

George laid his forehead on the steering wheel.

"Latex condoms," Richard said, still in that same booming voice. He turned around and tapped his son on the arm. "Hey, why didn't you put me up in one of those instead of shoving me away in that goddamn home?"

George chuckled. "No, Dad, a condom is a -"

"Oh, I know," Richard scoffed, waving his hand dismissively. "Christ fuck, I can't even have any fun with you anymore. If I wanted to sit in a car with a stick-in-the-mud I would've driven out to the Cove with your mother again."

George smiled, then went right back to leaning on the steering wheel. He threw an occasional glance into his rearview mirror but said nothing.

"Hey, you remember that summer I met Macy?" Richard giggled hoarsely, tapping him on the arm again.

George looked up, his brow so furrowed that there were deep torrents gouged in it. After a moment they loosened, and he smiled. "Oh, yeah. Yeah, of course."

"You were twenty-one and I told you not to make the same mistake I did. You were supposed to be damn near thirty before you brought anyone home and asked me what I thought of her."

"You liked her, though."

"She was eighteen. I liked her caboose."

"Dad!"

"What? I married your mom because she had an ass that wouldn't quit!"

"And?"

"It did," he grumbled, then played with the non-functioning power locks for a moment. "Anyway, she stood there in her jeans and her little black top and held her purse out in front of her like she was scared out of her mind."

"She was."

"And what did she have to be scared of, huh? What'd you go telling that girl to make her scared of meeting little old me?"

"Nothing but the truth, I swear," George laughed, finally falling back onto the chair. Several of the springs felt like they were about to dig into his back.

Richard looked thoughtful for a moment, staring out the windshield with a blank expression. "Man, she was beautiful though, wasn't she? Sweet too. Brought those presents for Charlotte and your sister. Except you didn't label which one was which and you said -"

"Said I didn't need to, hun, because you taught me how to tell them apart."

"The bigger one was for your sister, because she was the bigger one!" Richard finished, slapping himself on his boney knees. "Woo, did her face turn red! She didn't even say nothin', just sat there as red as a beet while we all had a good laugh at her."

"I think she figured you'd all hate her after that."

"Naw, she should've known better. She was a peach, always has been. Made you happy enough."

George was quiet again. He closed his eyes and felt the cushion of the seat against the back of his head and took a long, deep breath.

Richard watched him like that for a minute, then turned back toward his window. "Bargain Dentistry, walk-ins accepted," he mumbled after a moment.

George turned away from him, rolling his forehead along the steering wheel. It was beginning to leave a colourful smear across his head just under where his hair started, part red from the friction and part black from the shoe polish that had been used to make the wheel look presentable.

He stared at the smooth, green panel of the jeep beside him. Slowly, he raised his right hand and brought it up to where the keys dangled in the ignition. At first he didn't recognize the feel of them. They didn't have the surfboard keychain that Macy and Kerri had picked out for him at a truck stop while driving across Texas on his birthday several years before, nor were they weighed down with gas tabs, house keys, bike lock keys, padlock keys, the keys to the business, or the keys to every vehicle George had ever owned whether it was in running order or not. These weren't his keys, these were the rental keys. All that was on them was the one key which would both open the doors and start the ignition, as well as a leather ornament that said PADDLECOTT USED CARS AND RENTALS. Below it was a simple drawing of the bowtie the salesman had been wearing, polka-dots and all.

He took the key out of the ignition and clasped it in his hand, his index finger riding the smooth edge of it and turning it into a serrated claw. He held it like that for a moment, feeling the pressure of it and liking it, then opened his door and stepped out of the car.

Richard leaned down to watch him, his wrinkled old eyes barely visible under the brim of his cap. He said nothing.

The sun was hot and the air was cool. George turned around and looked at the Big Eight's parking lot, seeing only the gleaming tops of the cars parked there. There was nobody in sight, and they were far enough off the main drag that cars were few and far between. The check-in for the motel was in sight, but the clerk behind the counter was not. If he couldn't see the clerk, the clerk couldn't see him, as his father had always said.

"Never once did I say that," Richard mumbled.

There were no security cameras. Bad for business at a place like this, but good for George. Yes, very good indeed.

Satisfied that there were no eyes (human or electronic) watching him, he turned his attention back to the smooth green panel of the truck's passenger-side door. It shimmered and shone like a twisted funhouse mirror. He could see his reflection in it, distorted and malformed but him all the same. His hair was receding and there were lines under his eyes, not to mention a big black streak across his forehead. *Is that me?* he thought, turning from his reflection to the reflection of the Buick. The rental looked even smaller in the green-gray hue of the Jeep, like the dinkies he'd played with as a child. Vroom vroom vroom, time to get the car washed! Watch out for the suds! Vroom vroom vroom, now it's time to gas up! Don't forget to pay! Vroom vroom vroom!

Kerri had loved to play that with him. Macy had watched while washing dishes and smiled, only slightly.

The hand holding the key shook as he locked eyes with his gray-green reflection again. It was him, he decided. His mirror self, other self, dark self, whatever self. It had been a long time since he let it out to play but now it was time to do a little mischief. It had been years, but it wasn't like he forgot how. He swallowed hard, brought the key up, and pressed its glossy steel surface against the car.

He paused. A world of possibilities scattered over the surface of his mind like jacks over pavement, each one a fresh idea of what he could write. Bitch. Slut. Skank. Whore. Tramp. Or the always gratifying, simple squiggly line.

He pressed in on the key and felt as the jeep's panel bent it slightly until the pressure, distorting that demon-image of himself into weird greenish-gray swirls. His mouth was wet with anticipation. His heart pounded against his chest so hard that he could hear it in his ears. It was, in fact, all he could hear. If someone had seen him and snuck up from behind, he wouldn't have heard them until their hand was on his shoulder.

With that thought in mind he glanced over his shoulder out onto the parking lot. It was still empty.

Licking his lips, he gripped the key so tight that he felt its pattern press itself into the palm of his hand... then paused, the tension leaving his arm. His smile faded into a sad frown as his arm went limp and hit his side, keys clasped in it loosely.

He stared down at the mark he'd made, a white dot so tiny that he wasn't even sure if he could see it. He gawked at it madly, shifting focus from it to his reflection and then back again.

He put the key into his pocket, opened the door to the rented Buick, and got in with a sigh.

"You fucking pussy," came a gruff voice from the back, so full of anger that it startled George. "That was the most ridiculous thing I've ever seen."

George looked in the rearview mirror and saw Terrence Owchar sitting in the back seat. He was a massive bald man who took up the majority of the space in the back, his head scraping along the dirty plush roof of the car. He did not have eyebrows. What he had instead was a scowl that made his forehead come out like a caveman's, turning his eyes into beady pearls of white in a sea of black shadow. On either side of his mouth were the long ditches of frowns that had been worn not for days or months but for years. His face looked like a Thwomp from Super Mario Bros.

He stared at George from his reflection in the mirror, his gaze as unmoving as a stone.

"Oh, don't listen to him," Richard scoffed, waving a hand toward Terrence dismissively. "He was always trying to goad you into trouble. I'm proud of you. You're too old for that kind of rubbish."

"Bullshit you are. Fucking bullshit," Terrence snapped. "You remember that summer after Kerri was born? I know you do."

He did. He'd just been thinking about it.

They'd had a mutual friend named Roland who always had a bit of a crush on Macy. George had always thought it would go away once he and Macy had been together a while. Then he thought it would go away once they got married, then once they had Kerri... but it never did. One day around Christmas after a few drinks and a little pot, Roland had tried to kiss Macy. He hadn't gotten very far before she backed up and hit her head off the cabinet doing it.

"You didn't need me to goad you that night," Terrence said, snickering out of one side of his mouth. George could see his gums in the rearview, bright and pink at the bottom but blackened and dark around the edges of each tooth.

There was a sound from one of the motel rooms, he wasn't sure which, that made him look up. It had been like a scream. When he examined the doors again, they were still just doors and windows and curtains. Nothing had changed.

"That was different," Richard said matter-of-factly. His voice had become hoarse and he did not look at Terrence when he spoke, merely turned slightly in his direction. "Men do things when they're hurting like that... things that they'd never do normally. That's the thing to remember here, George, that she's hurting too."

"Whose side are you on, anyway?" Terrence urged, glaring at the old man.

It shut him up, at least for the moment.

"You still remember that night though, don't you? And not just the memory... the feeling. It felt so good. Better than anything else you've ever done, almost."

It was true. At the time, George pretended to laugh it off at first and had continued drinking until he could tell from Roland's expression that he had forgotten about it. The lot of them had gone out for a smoke around then, and slowly the others peeled away until it was just George and Roland left.

"What the fuck did you think you were doing?" George demanded, both his fists clenched. "Are you fucking retarded or something? What in Christ's name were you thinking?"

Roland tried a few times to explain, but it kept sounding stupid. The only thing that wouldn't sound stupid was the truth, and he wasn't about to say that.

Roland had had a bad knee for about a year at that point. He had fucked it up while working in a mine up in Kannibus and spent about three months walking with a cane and another four besides walking with a limp. George kicked it with everything he had and sent him scuttling to the ground in a twitching, yelling mess. Then, George started in on him. He'd mostly worked on the kidneys and the liver, but there were a few face shots too. Those were the ones he remembered best.

When he went back inside, Macy was waiting with a cold beer.

"For me?" he asked, smiling.

"For your hand," she frowned, placing the glass to his palm.

She was right. The cool condensation coming off the beer bottle soothed the hot, swelling digits of his hand. He could feel the muscles relaxing.

"You're not supposed to hit with a closed fist," she said, kissing him on the cheek.

"Heard that." He had smirked, flexing his fingers. "But it is at times hysterical."

In the front seat of the Buick, George laughed at the memory, his hand flexing against his calf the same way it had that night. He barely even realized he was doing it. The laugh felt strange and foreign to him, but still good. He held it as long as he could, not caring for the moment that his eyes were closed when he was supposed to be keeping watch.

"You see?" Richard said, piping up again after remaining quiet the whole way through the story. He turned around to look at Terrence and then back to George, his smile so large that it made his ears wiggle again. He slapped his knee. "You see what I was saying?"

The laughter was winding down now, and George wiped the smallest peck of moisture from his eye.

"She stood by you. You've done that and worse over the years and she stood by you. Maybe you should spend a little less time thinking about what she's done wrong and spend a little more time thinking about what you've done wrong."

George stopped and took a deep breath, then lay his head against the steering wheel again. He felt as though he were going to cry, but didn't. *Wanted* to cry even, but couldn't. Something in the back of his head kept stopping him and forcing the tears back. He thought about what a wonderful experience it would be to cry... a cathartic episode that might allow him to get through this. To weep out some of his horror and frustration and then leave it drying in the ripped seats of this condemnable rental car alongside the semen stains and soda splotches.

He opened his eyes and looked through the middle of the wheel at the motel again. There was a door with a letter on it, and then a large bay window with the curtains closed. They all still stood there in a row, completely unchanged, going on forever until they disappeared behind the greenish-gray jeep. The sun shone on them and shimmered all the metal doorknobs, creating a straight line of stars three feet above the cracked concrete walkway.

There was a door with a letter on it, and then a large bay window with the curtains closed.

He sighed, then shoved his hand into his pocket and withdrew it with the key and leather ornament again. He shoved it into the ignition and turned, holding it in place for a second until the engine roared to life.

Frowning, he slammed the car into reverse and took a deep breath.

He stopped.

There was a door with a letter on it, and then a large

bay window with the curtains closed.

The door was opening.

He shoved the car back into park immediately and cut the engine, then ducked down below the steering wheel.

The door to room 1C seemed to open of its own accord.

He held his breath without even realizing it, his face turning red.

Macy stepped out, her hair up in a bun with thin spidery locks coming down from it in all directions, framing her pale, beautiful face. He'd always loved when she wore her hair like that. It was very similar to the way she'd worn it on their wedding day.

She was wearing a pink dress that came down halfway to her knees and clung to her so tightly it was like she had been sewn into it, except around the breasts. It was loose on them, tottering this way and that against the tiny swells of her bosom. She carried a small black purse in one hand and had a gray jacket on over her shoulders, which she was just now pulling on.

She fixed her shoes. The heels hadn't been in the straps right.

She fixed her dress. It had bunched when she'd put it on.

She glowed in a way he hadn't seen in years.

A man came out of the room next. He was large, at least a foot over George who stood at a paltry five eight. He had a full head of hair that was swept to one side perfectly, even after the day's activities. He wore a nice suit that had to have been tailored, and shoes that looked to have cost more than the beaten-up Buick George was driving.

Macy started walking toward the jeep.

George ducked, making sure he was concealed by the dashboard.

The man stopped her, placing a gentle hand in the crook of her arm. He pulled her close to him and she fell into a kiss, holding it for a few seconds. She had to stand on her tip-toes to reach his lips.

They both smiled.

Their lips parted but their mouths stayed close, hers moving and saying something as her hand danced across his chest. She pushed it playfully.

George couldn't hear what she was saying, but knew it all the same.

Stop it, she had said, though she didn't want him to. She laughed coyly and sensually when she said it, patting him on the chest and using it as an excuse to touch the firm flesh. She'd done the same while they were dating, when he kissed her on her parent's couch with her father in the next room. She'd been both excited and scared by the possibility of getting caught.

The man smiled at her, and then the both of them made their way to the jeep. They sat in it for a moment, then the engine roared to life and they backed out.

George got out of the car again when they were pulling out of the parking lot and watched them as the pulled out onto the street. They did not look back and notice him.

He let out a deep sigh and got back in his empty car, then drove home alone.

BECOMING
CHAPTER FIVE

The morning light shone through his bedroom window, re-flecting off one of the cans of cheap orange soda in the case a few feet from his bed. It glimmered brightly in his eye, making him groan and roll over, only to find that she was right next to him. She looked as alert and beautiful and perfect as she always did, her big, dark eyes studying him with unmistakable interest.

"Good morning, sleepy head," Eve said lovingly. She wrapped her hands around his neck loosely, then moved in and gave him a quick peck on the lips.

"Is it morning already?" Adam groaned, glancing over his shoulder at the sun. "Fuck. How long were we up last night?"

"You've been asleep about five minutes," she admitted, trac-ing her fingers over the imperfections along his back. "I'm sorry if I woke you up, but I just couldn't get to sleep after all that... well, I'm sure you remember."

"How could I forget?" he chuckled, rolling over until he was on top of her, the covers and blankets twisting around their naked bodies.

She felt so smooth beneath him, her every touch setting fires *on his skin and making it scream for more of her. It was impossible to ever get enough. Just impossible. Her skin was so silky, her lips so sweet...*

"Baby!" she cried in pleasant surprise. "Again, already?"

He smiled, leaning in and kissing her.

Their lips met, and the sweet taste of strawberries rubbed off onto his tongue as her own came into his mouth, hot and fast, making his body tingle all over.

Suddenly, her eyes shot open and her nails dug into his side.

He opened his eyes and looked at her, saw the panic, and the fear. Their lips parted, but hers still moved trying to tell him something, trying to let him know. He drew back the hand that had been wrapped around her waist, and found that it was covered in blood. Silky, red blood that dribbled down his arm to his rolled-up sleeves.

"Aaah!" he screamed, pushing away from her.

"What?" she yelled, her eyes darting around the room in confusion. "What's wrong?"

"You..." he started, tears running down the sides of his face. "Eve, you were dead..."

She smiled, drawing his head down onto her breast and brushing her fingers through his short, dark hair. "Oh, sweetie... sweetie, no. It was just a dream."

"No, no it's not. It's not a dream, you're dead. You're not really here."

"Shh, shh, just listen." she told him, forcing him to keep his head on her chest as his hot tears spilled out onto her breasts.

He obeyed, stopping to listen to her.

But she said nothing.

"Honey?" he asked, confused.

"Shh," she chided him, pushing his head back into place.

He sighed, and for a minute there was nothing. Then, out of nowhere, he heard it, wondering how he hadn't before.

Bump-Bump.

Bump-Bump.

Bump-Bump.

It was her heart, beating for him, just for him, pumping the love that she felt for him through her entire body.

"Hear that?" she asked.

He nodded.

"See, I'm alive. I'm okay. Really, Adam, I'm fine."

"It just seemed so real."

"But it wasn't."

"I love you."

She smiled at him, bringing him back up to give her a kiss. "I love you, too... but are you ever going to take this out?"

He looked down.

The end of a blade was sticking out of Eve's chest, blood pumping out onto their sheets and mattress. The point protruded from between her breasts so far that he didn't know how he hadn't felt it or been impaled on it as they'd rolled around between the sheets. The bed around her was filled with blood.

"Oh my God!" he yelled, even as the blade thrust forward, stabbing into him as well and stapling the both of them together. He screamed.

"I love you," his lover mouthed, and he as well. As the both of them kissed and embraced once more, the bed itself became a massive set of lips and teeth, closing over them and swallowing.

Big, red eyes opened as its tongue whipped out and licked its lips.

"Just like mother used to make," *the creature chuckled, laughing at his own little joke.*

ᛉ

In his hospital bed, somewhere in his subconscious, Adam Genblade heard the shrill beat of his heart monitor.

Beep, beep.

Beep, beep.

Beep, beep.

Somewhere, deep inside his heart of hearts, the sound brought him some sense of peace.

BECOMING
CHAPTER SIX

Xander brought his lighter to his lips to light his cigarette, only to realize that he already had a lit one in his mouth. Huffing at his own stupidity, he placed the unused smoke carefully into his pack, then took a long haul off of his current one.

"I thought you were quitting," Mike said, strolling up to him from across the school yard. Mike knew exactly where to find Xander doing exactly what he was doing now, by the large brick wall that faced Eastman street. The of the road was blocked by a high chain link fence and a collection of alder trees that were bare of leaves this time of year. It had become the undisputed smoking section of Coral Beach high.

"Shut up," Xander responded, blowing smoke in his friend's face.

"Fine," Mike conceded, raising his hands in defeat. "But just because you've got a healing factor, doesn't mean you have to poison the rest of us, you know."

"Nut nust necause nou not na nealing nactor... blah

blah blah," Xander mimicked, extinguishing his smoke in the ground next to him. He sat for a minute, a determined look on his face, as though he were bracing himself. Suddenly, he threw his head back, slamming it against the wall as hard as he could.

"Ow! Fuck!" he cursed. He brought his hands up to the already expanding welt on the back of his head, hissing as his touch brought new pain to it. "Fuck fuck fuck."

"Feel better?" Mike asked calmly.

"A little," he said, rubbing the back of his skull. "You know, for a second."

"How many times have you done that?" he asked, leaning over to examine the blood smear against the wall.

"Oh, fifty or sixty. It starts to take my mind off things after about ten tries, but then I start to bleed and the healing factor kicks in, so I have to start all over again."

"Dude... you need help," Mike chuckled, finding a morbid humor in his friend's words.

"No," Xander corrected, shaking his finger. "What I need is for life to stop slapping me when I'm not looking. At least when it's the wall, I know when it's coming. But standing around like a doof waiting for something bad to happen... that makes you crazy."

"No, the fact that you actually used the word doof in a sentence makes you crazy."

Xander did not smile, instead opting to reach for his cigarette pack and pull out another smoke. He lit it quickly, snapping the lighter shut again to douse the flame and then pocketing both it and the half empty pack.

"Didn't you just finish one?" Mike asked, giving the paper cylinder a disgusted look.

"No, I just started one. Pay attention," he drawled, taking a few short puffs to make sure that it was lit. His eyes glazed in relaxation as the smoke traveled down his throat and into his lungs, and he held it in as long as he could stand before exhaling again.

"Fine then, be that way. All I wanted to do was talk."

"No, Cathy told you to come out and talk to me the first chance you had to get me alone," he snapped, turning to glare at his friend for the first time in the entire conversation.

"How did you-?"

"Super. Human. Senses."

"Right," Mike nodded. "Sorry. Didn't mean to patronize you or anything."

"No harm. No foul."

"Seriously, though. You wanna tell me what's on your mind?"

"Nothing," Xander said quickly, giving his head a little shake.

Mike leaned forward, looking around to the other side of Xander, where there was a pile of no less than ten cigarette butts and growing. "You maybe wanna try that one again?"

Xander exhaled through both nostrils.

"Look," Mike started, sitting down next to Xander and folding his large hands together. "I know that this thing with Julie is rough. And that it sucks. But, if there's one thing I learned from that massive fight Cathy and I had, it's that -"

"It's not Julie," Xander interjected, waving his smoke in dismissal, sending tiny tendrils of smoke into the air.

"What, then?"

Xander sighed, leaning his head back against the wall and staring forward into the gray sky. "I think... I think I was in Genblade's dream last night."

There was a long pause as Mike glanced back and forth. "You mean... you had a dream about Genblade."

"No, I mean Genblade was having a nightmare and I was there somehow," he explained in an 'isn't-it-obvious' kind of tone that made him sound even more insane.

"Ooookaaay..." Mike stretched, his eyes widening. "I'm trying to follow you here, buddy, but you're going to have to help me out. Let's just say for argument's sake that that's actually possible. How exactly would you know this was Genblade's dream? Did you take a wrong turn, end up walking out his ear and go: 'Hey, this isn't my head'?"

Xander laughed, coughing up smoke. "No. No, I know it was Genblade's dream because I was the bad guy. It was from his point of view. It was all about me killing Spider for no apparent reason, which is, I'm sure, the way he sees it."

"All right," Mike interrupted so that Xander would be quiet. "Again, assuming that were possible... Genblade's comatose, man. He is experiencing no brain activity. It's not like he's asleep or something, so the guy is not waking up. The doctors said so."

"Have you met the doctors in this town?"

"In any case, Adam Genblade is *brain dead*, okay?"

"What about the brain stem? There's no way of knowing how all of the chemicals and crap in Genblade's system affect him. His consciousness may somehow be buried in his..."

Mike gave Xander a look.

"I'm reaching a bit far, aren't I?"

"Yes," Mike said bluntly. Then he continued, more softly. "But then, a week ago I was about to kill you when I was interrupted by some freak that used crystal gems to tell the future. So, we'll be giving you the benefit of the doubt on this one."

Xander smiled, placing the butt of his smoke between his thumb and forefinger and flicking it over the nearby wire mesh fence. "It wasn't even so much the dream, really," Xander began, his words jumbling together as he got more and more worked up. "I woke up from it easily enough. But in the middle of the night. With no blood, it just..."

"The Womb's an animal, and animals don't just change their behavior like that for no good reason," Mike nodded.

"Right!" Xander breathed, glad that someone was articulate enough to voice what he had been thinking. "Exactly right!"

Mike was thoughtful for a moment. "It could be the snow. You never know, the Womb might behave differently in winter."

Xander shot him a look. "Every time we make excuses for my other half acting all wonky..."

"Somebody dies. I know." Mike groaned. "Besides, I feel it too. I woke up a couple of times last night. Once I even fell out of bed. Cathy was saying the same thing. We can all feel it. It's a... a..."

"A change in the wind," Xander finished.

"Yeah."

"Like the weather felt it too, and thought it was time to snow, but really it was just something coming. Something big. Something drastic."

"I'm sure it's nothing."

"I'm sure it's not," Xander grumbled sarcastically, lighting another smoke.

Mike snatched it away and was about to break it in half when he brought it to his own lips instead, taking a long drag.

Xander stared at him, then pulled out another cigarette and lit it.

"What do you think's going to happen?" Mike asked, taking short but relaxing drags.

"I don't know," Xander admitted somberly. "But I think we've both been down this road too many times to expect something good."

BECOMING
CHAPTER SEVEN

Mandy Peterson awoke suddenly, her eyelids clicking softly as they snapped open. At first, she wasn't quite sure where she was as she looked up at an off-white stucco ceiling. Her heart rate raced so quickly that she could hear it pounding in her ears.

"That was a good session," said Dr. Warren O'Toole from where he sat perched on his chair across the room. He was still scribbling notes on the sheet of paper attached to his clipboard, his hand going a mile a minute.

"It seems like I just closed my eyes," she said groggily as she sat up and put her hair back in a ponytail, pushing it away from her cute, plump face. Her cheeks were perfect and smooth, except for a few teenage blemishes and a small M-shaped scar on her forehead that she'd had since birth. Her sweater kept her warm on this chilly day, so big on her that it only stopped halfway between her hips and her knees. It made her look innocent and sweet, two words that anyone who really knew her would probably not use to describe her.

"You always say that," he grinned from behind his large round glasses, pushing the bangs of his black hair back and shoving his pocket watch into his breast pocket. His hand was covered by a red and white handkerchief. He stood up, revealing himself to be a tall, lanky man, his arms straggly yet strong. "It's the truest sign of a good session."

"And you always say that," she pointed out, smiling at him just a little.

She used to despise these hypnosis psychology sessions but had begun to find them quite relaxing. She even looked forward to them from time to time.

"So, when will you need to see me again?" she asked, stretching wide and then sighing happily.

"Hmm?" O'Toole hummed, lost in some stray thought. "Oh, yes. I'm sorry... um, let's say next week sometime. Contact me on Friday and we'll see when's a good time for you, okay?"

She shrugged the way only a fourteen year old can.

"Whatever," she chirped, then turned toward the door.

Warren watched her leave, then collapsed back into his chair, visibly exhausted.

"Oh, God..." he mumbled as reached behind his desk and pulled out a bottle of Jack Daniels and a short, wide glass. Throwing his clipboard into the nearest open cabinet, he poured himself a drink.

"Once more into the breach, my friends..." he murmured, downing the contents of the glass as fast as he could. "We few... we happy few."

Julie Peterson walked through the halls of Coral Beach High School, well aware of the fact that she was being watched. Stared at. Some even gawked, but mostly just those who rode the little bus to school and simply didn't know better, in her opinion.

She didn't mind either way.

She was more than used to being looked at, talked about, and secretly sworn upon. It had been happening to her for her entire life, and today was no exception. Except for the fact that today, they all had a good reason to stare.

Her shirt was loose on her and not at all appropriate for the weather outside. It was bright purple and came down across her arms in long, open sleeves. The neck was ruffled and bunched so much that it looked like she had a scarf on with it, although the material was so airy it wouldn't have provided any insulation. It was much more conservative than her usual attire, and she'd almost decided to not wear it several times that morning. In the end, the choice had come down to one simple fact:

It was one of his favorites.

The rest of her ensemble, her makeup, even her jewelry had been chosen on similar merits, right down to the choice not to conceal the freckles that dotted her cheeks. He'd always said he thought they were cute.

She stormed down the halls, her eyes filled with a grim determination and a spite that had become her trademark. Coming into the lobby, she took a long look around at who was standing around in the pre-class crowd. After just a moment, she spotted her prey.

Xander Drew sat in one corner, his eyes far off and distant. Mike Harris, Cathy Kennessy, Tommy Irons and Julie's her cousin, Mandy Peterson, all stood near him, talking about something stupid no doubt. He seemed oblivious to the rest of them.

She walked right up to them.

Cathy noticed her first, her eyes growing wide.

Julie tapped Xander twice on the shoulder.

Slowly, Xander turned around to face his girlfriend. He knew it was her before he even saw her just by the smell of her perfume and that feeling he got in the pit of his stomach when she was close by. He smiled at her. She had sparkling green eyes and freckles that ran across her cheeks and the bridge of her nose no matter how much lemon juice she applied to them. Her hair was never the same way twice, always highlighted differently so that she was always fresh, always new, always beautiful.

"Hi," he said simply when he realized that he was staring at her.

She smiled, then leaned in and opened her mouth. She kissed him in front of everyone, her tongue going in and out of their view as it darted between his mouth and her own, her hands traveling a mile a minute as they danced everywhere over him, squeezing him closer, grabbing at his muscular arms and abdomen. Her lips were soft, so soft, and yet the way she used them was so hard and powerful that it made his head swim, hard to think.

She broke off the kiss and stepped back, leaving him and every other person around awestruck. She smiled at him, tilting her head to one side and letting her hair fall over her shoulder in a way he'd always found adorable.

"Xander..." she said softly, soothingly. "... It's over."

With that she spun on her heels and started to walk away toward the front doors.

"Julie!" Xander called, shaking off the effects of her kiss and taking off after her. He almost tripped once, still lightheaded.

Cathy cringed as she watched the event, wanting to close her eyes and yet completely unable to, like the way people stopped to watch car wrecks. Even though you'd have nightmares for a week, you just couldn't miss it. Mike squeezed her hand tight, frowning. She did the same.

Mandy shook her head and sighed, looking as though her eyes might soon well up with tears.

Tommy just stood there, dumbfounded. After a moment, he elbowed Mike. "Did you see that kiss?"

Mike rolled his eyes.

"Julie, wait!" Xander called again, catching up to her as she neared the exit and taking her by the arm.

"Get your fucking hands off me!" she screamed loudly, whirling around and drawing the attention of anyone who wasn't already watching.

Warren O'Toole stopped talking to Principal Schneider, turning around and cocking an eyebrow at the scene.

Xander obeyed, letting her go immediately. "I'm sorry, I just... what was that, Julie?"

"That was a break up," she said matter-of-factly. "A damn good one, if you ask me. Just ask any girl here outside of Cathy and Mandy, and I'm sure they'll agree."

"Can't we talk about this?" Xander whispered between clenched teeth, very aware of the crowd.

"I've done all the talking I was going to do, Xander, but if you wanna talk... fine! Let's talk!" she yelled, shoving him back a pace. "Let's talk about the way you started off by rejecting me time and time again, making me feel like crap! Huh? Or, would you rather talk about all the ways I tried to be everything you wanted, and every time I did, you changed what you wanted! Or maybe..." she snarled, pointing toward Cathy. "Maybe we can talk about your little crush on her, hmm? Come on... everybody else is!"

The crowds gaze shifted momentarily from Julie to Cathy, who tried her best not to lock eyes with any one of them. Mike smiled at her, and suddenly she didn't care what they thought.

"Julie, please," Xander pleaded, his eyes filled with hurt. "Julie, don't do this. I thought you said you -"

"Yeah? Well, I don't. Guess you're not the only one here who can change their mind, huh?"

She snarled at him, then turned to walk away. This time he made no effort to stop her, just watching her hips swing from side to side in a triumph, even if that triumph was over him.

She reached out to open the door, when suddenly it swung open hard and fast, catching her in the nose. Blood spewed forth from it as she fell back, hitting the tiled floor like a ton of bricks, scraping her hand as she did so.

The door cracked against the wall, shattering the plaster there and sending small chips to the floor.

Ian Char and Duncan Combs stepped into the school, their big, black hiking boots making long streaks on the floor. Ian looked down at the bleeding Julie and smacked his lips at her, giving her a quick double kiss before reaching into the front of his pants and pulling out a gun. Duncan followed suit, pulling two similar handguns from behind him, aiming at nobody in particular but causing everyone in the room to scream nonetheless. On each of their right arms was a bright red tattoo of the letter T, their sleeves ripped off to accent it, hiding it from no one anymore.

"What the hell?" Mike swallowed, taking a long step forward. Cathy pulled him back. Taking note of the guns, he nodded.

Xander clenched his fists. The Womb organ swelled up inside him, the beast banging at the doors, ready to explode from his veins and take them down.

He suppressed it.

There were too many people around who would see, and Julie might get hurt if there was a firefight. He took a step forward, leaning down to pull on Julie's shoulder.

From between Ian and Duncan, Randy Owchar stepped into the school, brandishing a shotgun and his very own Tee tattoo.

Xander quickly got Julie to her feet and back into the crowd, where Tommy's teeth could be heard clenching above the screaming and yelling. Randy had killed Tommy's best friend, Sud, in order to gain entry into the Tees. He'd shot him in cold blood in this very hall.

Randy noticed Xander and aimed his gun directly at him.

"Hold it!" he bellowed, although his voice didn't really suit his attitude. Not deep enough. Not that anyone was going to argue the point with him while he was brandishing a sawed-off shotgun.

Xander froze immediately, raising his hands in the air. *I might... might be able to survive a blast at this range, depending on where it hit, but there was no guarantee that nobody else would get hit either.*

"Turn around," Randy ordered.

Xander complied, biting his lip because he knew he could take down that son of a bitch child-killer in ten seconds flat.

"Well, well, well," Randy smiled, shaking his head at Xander. He lowered his voice considerably, so that only he and Xander could hear. "If it isn't the Black Womb."

Slowly, Xander's eyes went wide, as he started to realize what that feeling he'd had was all about...

BECOMING
CHAPTER EIGHT

Alone in the dark, Adam Genblade scuttled around, look-ing, waiting, watching. There were voices in the dark, he would swear on it. He thought that he recognized them, but he just couldn't pin them down. He knew... he knew that he had to find them though. Something very bad would happen if he didn't. He was warm, but there was a cold breeze. There were sticky things stuck to him all over, but he couldn't see what they were.

"Honey?" *Eve said, and Adam opened his eyes quickly.*

"What?" *he blurted, turning away from the road just long enough to look at her.* "What is it, sweetie?"

She gave him a look that was both angered and disappoint-ed.

"You're falling asleep," *she huffed, crossing her arms.*

"I am not!" *he protested.*

"I was just watching you. You were falling asleep!"

"I was just resting my eyes!"

"That's the same god damn thing!" *She almost smiled at how feebly he was arguing, but tried to resist it. She couldn't smile, that would only encourage him.*

He caught the grin, smiling back. *"We'll stop at the next gas bar and get something to eat, I'll rest up a bit, and then we'll grab some coffee and get on the road again, okay?"*

"Yeah. There's a McDonald's only a mile away."

"I didn't see that sign."

"Maybe because you were asleep."

"Yes, dear."

"Oh, don't you yes dear me..."

The highway McDonald's was cleaner than most, most likely due to the frequent hungry businessmen and travelers that came through. You never can tell when someone important enough to know the head health inspector in the country would just walk in and order a Big Mac.

Eve walked over to a booth seat and sat down, shooting a smile at Adam. "You know what I want, right?"

His eyes went up into his head as he regurgitated the order that she'd always made for the last seven years. "A quarter pounder with cheese, no mayo, no onions. Large fries. Side order of six-piece nuggets and one fajita. And a Coke."

"Diet Coke." she corrected.

"I knew that," he said, waving a finger at her lovingly.

"You did not."

"I did," he repeated, blowing her a kiss as he stepped up to order.

At the desk was a cute little blonde number with hips that were shaped like an hourglass and large breasts. He didn't mean to notice that she had breasts, but found he couldn't help it. He didn't think she was wearing a bra. Her name tag, which he read aloud to cover up the fact that he had been gawking at this young girl's tits, said 'Sara'.

She looked him up and down, tilted her hips to one side and licked her lips. "May I take your order, please?"

"Uh..." Adam stuttered, trapped in the girl's big, blue eyes. He realized that she could not possibly be one day over sixteen. "Um... I'll have a... a double Big Mac meal, please. With Coke."

"Would you like that super-sized? I know I would," she said, winking playfully at him.

"Um... no, thanks," he gulped.

"Will there be anything else?"

"No. Yes! My... my wife, she'll have a quarter pounder with cheese, no mayo, no onions. Large fries. Side order of six-piece nuggets and one fajita. And a Coke."

"By the looks of her, she should be getting a Diet Coke," Sara muttered under her breath.

"Yes!" Adam realized, almost yelling. "Yes, she'll have a Diet Coke!"

Sara smiled at him, again looking him up and down. "That'll be fifteen eighty eight, please."

He reached into his pocket and pulled out a twenty, unfolded it, then handed it to her. As she took it, she rubbed her finger against his thumb. He jerked away fast, and she smiled, passing him his change.

The meal went without incident. Eve gobbled up her quarter pounder like there was no tomorrow, then slowly ate her fajita and nuggets, like always. He was done everything before she even started eating the fries, so he decided that he would step outside for a cigarette. Giving his wife a kiss, he left the building and headed out back.

He pulled a smoke out of his jacket pocket and brought it to his lips, then began patting himself to find his lighter.

"Here," came a voice from behind him.

He turned quickly to see Sara sitting against the brick wall behind him, halfway through a smoke of her own, handing a butane lighter to him. The top three buttons of her shirt were undone, showing off an insane amount of cleavage. Her breasts were so large, and smooth... and now Adam realized that not only was there no bra, but no tan line either.

"Uh, thank you," he said, his hand shaking as he took the lighter.

Again, she looked him up and down. She got up, stepping toward him.

"Excuse me..." he started, but didn't finish, unsure of how to act as she continued to back him up until his back was against the wall.

She unbuttoned her pants quickly, grabbed his wrist and forced his hand onto her crotch. She was strong, stronger than she looked, and Adam could not pull away. Her other hand reached down and grabbed him between the legs, squeezing it tightly, longingly, the way Eve had not since they were teenagers. Before Adam knew what was happening, she was kissing him passionately on the lips, despite his very real efforts to stop her. She forced his hand down inside her pink panties with the rose in front and he felt her warmth, smooth and wet. He felt the warmth melt away his ability to resist, and he found his fingers doing things that he wished they would not.

"Sara!" came an angry voice from behind them, and the girl quickly turned around. There, standing with the sun against his back making him appear to be aflame with anger, was Xander Drew. "What the fuck are you doing slutting around again? How many times do I have to tell you, you're my girlfriend?"

"I'm not your girlfriend!" Sara screamed, tears flowing down her cheeks even as he descended upon her. "I never was!"

"Oh, you are and you will be!" Xander bellowed, grabbed her by the arm and pulling her forward into a kiss.

She bit his lip, drawing blood.

"Bitch!" he screamed, drawing back and punching her as hard as he could between her legs.

"Ahh!" she screamed, blood soaking through her pants as she bent over in pain.

It was only now that Adam noticed that the boy had a concealed knife in his hand. He had just stabbed the young woman in the privates.

"Oh my God!" Adam yelped, backing himself against the wall again.

Xander turned from Sara, her body raked with sobs and screams, as if only just now noticing Adam. "What the fuck do you want, pops? What were you doing with my girl anyway?"

"Please, I'm a tourist. I'm from Texas. Really, I... I really don't understand what's going on here, sir."

"Shut up, hick," Xander scoffed. "Fucking Texas hick."

"Please, I -"

"Adam?" came a voice like springtime. Both men turned to see Eve standing by the corner, her last chicken nugget in her hand. "Adam, what's going on?"

"Eve, for god's sake, go inside!" Adam barked.

"No, no," Xander smiled. "You got to have a go with my woman... only fair that I get to have a go with yours..."

"What's he talking about, Adam?" Eve asked, hurt in her voice. Then she noticed Sara, clinging to life against the wall as blood soaked her jeans right down to her knees. "Oh my God..."

"Don't worry, baby." Xander smiled evilly, holding up his blade. "It'll hurt, but it probably won't hurt that much if you're good."

"No!" Eve screamed, turning to run.

Adam lunged for Xander, who slashed out with the blade, slicing through Eve's tender flesh. She went down, hitting her head off the sidewalk and breaking her nose.

"No!" Adam yelled, crying himself by now.

"Fucker!" Xander yelled, kicking Adam in the ribs as he got to his feet. "That's two of my good fucks you've ruined in ten god damn minutes."

Adam coughed, trying desperately to get his breath.

Xander smiled. "That's okay, though. I'm in the mood to eat something else, now..."

Adam turned around. In one horrifying instant, he realized he was no longer standing next to Xander Drew, but the thing from his nightmare back in the car. The Darkness. The Black Womb. A massive, hulking creature made of black ooze that clung to him with hate and loathing. The demon's claws twitched, ready to rip off flesh for it to eat. Its mouth dislocated like a snake's, to fit more of Adam past those big, filed teeth of his.

"Black Womb lives!" the creature snarled as it leapt down upon Adam, biting into his jugular and ripping it away. As he died, out of the corner of his eye, he saw Eve twitch with life.

"Don't worry, man," the Womb assured him. "She'll be joining you as soon as I'm done with her..."

Adam blacked out then, hearing only the beginning of his wife's scream before he passed out.

BECOMING
CHAPTER NINE

Xander stared at Randy Owchar, their gazes equal in their rage and ferocity, neither of them moving for a full minute. His heart was beating a mile a second, a thousand thoughts going through his head at once, but only one loud enough for him to actually hear:

How does he know who I am?

Xander's left eye twitched with unreleased anger, his tongue moving as if to say words that he knew he could not in a mouth as dry as a desert.

Randy smiled. He'd shaved his head since Xander had last seen him, in an obvious attempt to look more like the leader of the Tees, Roulette. Roulette, a murdering, child-molesting skinhead that sucked in young boys and turned them into killers with the coldness and effectiveness of a factory, and one of the Womb's greatest enemies. And Randy's idol. And now Randy knew who the Black Womb was.

Randy moved forward, his leather vest ruffling. There were two handguns shoved into the front of his ripped jeans and a red bandanna sticking out of one pocket. He looked as though he was trying to grow a beard, the effect of which was a very patchy five o'clock shadow. His eyes were still blue, but they seemed beadier now, narrower since he'd killed Sud.

He pointed the gun directly at Xander's head.

He motioned to Ian, Duncan, and eight other Tees that had gathered in behind them, each of them sporting a Tee tattoo. He recognized one of them as George Walker, the father of Kerri Walker. Kerri had been killed by Zakron, the Anti-Womb, along with God only knew how many other people.

I guess now we know why the Tees wanted to help find Kerri so much, thought Mike from back in the corner. As he slowly took a step forward, Tommy followed his lead. Cathy pulled Mandy back.

"Find the Omega-Slut," Randy demanded, and Duncan and Ian immediately started searching through the crowd, their guns pointing at everyone they passed. "The rest of you, get on crowd control. I don't want any stragglers."

Cathy's eyes went wide as she realized who they were talking about. Mandy had been living in Coral Cove until a few months ago, where she'd dated a member of a rival gang called the Omegas. He'd branded her as one of 'their' girls, which caused serious trouble when she'd first moved to Coral Beach. Randy had tried to kill her to gain entry into the Tees.

"We have to get out of here," she whispered harshly to Mandy.

"No!" Mandy protested, pulling away from the older girl. "We have to stay here with Mike! He'll look after us!"

"What are you talking about?"

"Stop pretending you don't know what I'm talking about!" Mandy demanded, a little too loudly.

Randy smirked at Xander, now that it was just the two of them near. "All these months, it's been you... hasn't it? Ever since that first Tee got the crap beat out of him by the Black Shadow back in September when he was trying to get some action... that was you, wasn't it?"

Xander stood tight lipped, squinting his eyes.

"Now that I know it, I can't see how I didn't see it. It's in the eyes... even though they're so different, you can see all that anger in your eyes, Womb."

"And what do you see right now, asshole?" Xander whispered, speaking for the first time since the whole ordeal started.

Randy chuckled. "Fear. Because you know what's happening here. And you know you can't stop it. Just like you couldn't stop me from pumping eighty-seven cents worth of hot lead into Sud."

"You're going to die, Randy," Xander promised, his nails digging into his own palms so hard they drew blood. "I'll find you. I'll hunt you down. After having you this close, and me this mad, you think I'll ever forget your scent? The only chance you got at living is if you start running, right now, and never stop."

Randy smiled, quickly pointing his gun to the side and firing, blowing both barrels in a seventh grade girl's face. She flew back onto the floor, her flesh, blood, and brain matter spread across the wall in a large V-shape.

Everyone screamed, and Xander's eyes went wide with shock. He turned to lunge at Randy, onto to discover he had the gun pointed at another girl.

"I'll kill one of them for every threat you make, little man," Randy assured him politely, a childish glint of glee in his eyes.

Xander said nothing, keeping unbroken eye contact with the killer.

"Good boy," Randy chimed approvingly.

A young blond boy that Mike recognized as Dwayne Piercey stepped between him and Tommy. The kid had light brown eyes that betrayed how scared and determined he was, a dangerous combination in someone holding a gun. He had a scar on his upper lip and wore a backward baseball cap. His tattoo looked fresh... earlier that day fresh. Mike gave Tommy a look and a wink, who nodded.

"Hey!" came Ian's voice, from the back.

Mike's eyes darted in that direction as he realized that the bastard had found them.

"I got her!" Ian yelled, pulling Cathy out of the crowd and throwing her to the floor. An Omega tattoo stood out in bright red on her arm.

Randy raised an eyebrow, throwing a glance at Duncan.

"That's not her!" Duncan screamed, slapping Ian alongside his head. He picked up Cathy and threw her against the blood spattered wall, her red pen falling out of her jeans pocket onto the floor with a clack.

Cathy smirked devilishly, licking her thumb and bringing it to the tat, wiping the corner of it off. "Gotcha."

"Bitch!" Ian screamed, raising his gun to her.

At that moment, Mike and Tommy both turned on Dwayne, each of them kicking his feet out from underneath him. Mike drew back and kicked Dwayne's wrist, sending the gun skidding across the floor, lost in the crowd of horrified onlookers.

Duncan turned to where Ian had discovered Cathy just in time to see Mandy take off toward the rear exits.

"Fuck," he whispered. He raised both his handguns toward the crowd, who immediately parted to get out of the line of fire, inadvertently giving him a clear shot at Mandy.

Cathy kicked Duncan in the kneecap, and the shot shattered the trophy case instead of hitting Mandy.

"Slut!" Duncan cursed, turning the barrel toward Cathy, his teeth gritting as he seethed.

"Watch it!" Tommy said, slamming him over the back of the head with both fists. "Or somebody might get the impression that you're a woman-hating murderer."

Cathy smiled up at him as he helped her up.

Randy's eyes went wide as he saw the scene that was playing out before him. Most of his Tees were either frozen stiff or engaged with unarmed children. Grunting, he stepped forward and took aim at Mandy with the shotgun.

Spurt!

He opened both eyes and looked down, seeing Xander's hand pressed against his arm, but couldn't figure out why it hurt so bad... until Xander withdrew, revealing that there had been four claws at the end of each finger, each one now covered in his blood. In his other hand,

Xander held a small, curved dagger with a hilt that had been carved into the shape of a dragon.

"Now who's scared?" Xander quipped. He jumped backward, ducked, then propelled himself forward into Randy, tackling his legs as they both went down.

George Walker squinted, watching as Tommy, Cathy, and Mike all engaged various Tees, while Xander was trying to wrestle Randy's gun away from him without success as the two of them rolled around on the floor. He turned, catching something out of the corner of his eye, then smiled to himself and raised his gun.

Mike punched Ian in the face, sitting atop his chest and wailing on him relentlessly, throwing off the Tees that were trying to pull him off of their compatriot.

"Son of a bitch!" he bellowed, spittle flying from his lips. "Think you can come in here and pull this shit? I'll rip your face off!"

Sven Douglas, a small, middle-aged balding Tee with buck teeth, pointed a gun at Mike.

Mike immediately got up as if to surrender, then backhanded the gun away, lashing out with a strong punch with his other hand.

"It's not nice to point," he whispered, turning back and kicking Ian again before turning to another Tee.

Cathy was kicking Duncan in the ribs repeatedly, trying to make sure he stayed down, swearing at him and his mother with every blow, sweat pouring off her brow as she worked off months of anger and frustration aimed at her oppressors.

Tommy took on a Tee he knew from grade school named Justin Langley, who had beaten him up once in grade three. He found it gave him a remarkable sense of closure, a justified smile across his lips.

"Gimmie *your* lunch money!" he yelled at the confused man as he pounded another blow into his skull.

Xander pinned both of Randy's arms to the floor, inches away from the pre-teenage girl that Randy had so callously murdered just moments before, her blood sticking to his leather vest.

"Killer!" he spat angrily, digging his claws into Owchar's hand. "I should give you death! You deserve death!"

His eyes began to darken as his pupils expanded, the true Womb organ in his gut pumping fiercely against Xander's will, trying with all its might to burst free.

"You should talk!" Randy retorted, kneeing Xander in the gut.

Xander let go in shock, allowing Randy to kick him off.

"I should have killed you when I had the chance!" he bellowed in the Womb's voice, echoing off the lobby walls.

Randy scrambled with his weapon and pointed it at Xander, who batted it away and slashed at the killer with the blade in his opposite hand. Randy reached for one of the guns held in his pants, drawing and pointing it directly at Xander.

Xander grabbed him by the wrist, digging his claws in deep and pulling forward. He dropped the dragon blade and snatched up the gun, turning it on its owner.

For the first time, Randy's eyes were filled with fear instead of hatred as Xander pulled back the hammer on the gun and placed first pressure on the trigger.

"Everybody stop!"

All parties turned in the direction of the voice.

Xander's resolve melted in an instant as his eyes found Julie's.

Her arm was held tightly by George Walker, the tip of his gun pressed forcefully against her dimpled cheek.

BECOMING
CHAPTER TEN

Walker smiled, taking a deep whiff of Julie's hair as she cringed away, blood still streaming from her nose.

"She seems nice, Xander," he said soothingly, turning toward the boy. "Put down your weapon, or I'll kill her."

Xander stared at Julie for a long moment, and she back at him. A blood vessel had broken in her left eye, but she still looked so beautiful. So fragile. Letting out a deep breath, he dropped the gun to the floor with a clang that momentarily shattered the silence that Walker had created in the room.

Randy picked up the weapon quickly and aimed it at Xander's head.

"Put up your hands," Walker demanded, pushing the gun tighter against Julie.

She yelped when the metal touched her temple, just loud enough to be heard.

Xander took but a second to retract his claws, then complied with Walker's demands as the blackness drained from his eyes.

"Now tell your friends to do the same."

He shot a sorrowful glance at Mike. He, Cathy, and Tommy all reluctantly raised their hands.

"Fuck," Mike groaned as Ian sprung to life, taking one of Duncan's guns and aiming at his ear.

Xander grimaced at Walker. "If only your daughter could see you now," he whispered, shaking his head.

"Watch it," Walker snapped, pulling back the hammer on the gun. "Or they'll have a plastic bag for each one of your bitch's brain cells. What would that be, two?"

"Xander, please..." Julie pleaded, tears mixing with the blood on her face.

Xander bit his lip, and did not respond to Walker's taunts.

"Good." Walker smiled. "Now, Omega-Slut!" he called out to the crowd, turning to face them. "I know you're still here! I can smell a cover from a mile away!"

From the crowd, there was nothing.

"You don't show yourself, I'll make paper-maché out of her skull!" he threatened, squeezing Julie's arm until she made a painful sound.

"No, no, no, no..." Cathy repeated to herself, her eyes darting over the crowd.

"All right," Walker sighed, putting his finger on the trigger.

"Wait!"

Xander closed his eyes and cursed to himself. When he opened them, Mandy Peterson was stepping slowly out of the crowd.

"Don't do this," he whispered to Randy without daring to turn and face him. "It doesn't have to be this way.

I've got friends - Tim White, in the FBI - I can get you a deal if you end this now, Randy."

"Shut up," Randy sneered.

"I know you aren't a bad person..."

"Shut up!" Randy yelled, firing a shot past Xander's head and striking someone in the arm. He didn't see who it was, but they fell into the crowd and disappeared. His screams rang out across the hall though.

Again, Xander bit his lip, this time so hard that it bled.

"You can't trick me again," he warned, the gun shaking. "You can't."

Ian and Duncan stepped up, each of them grabbing one of Mandy's arms. Ian pulled up Mandy's sleeve and examined the Omega tattoo on her right shoulder blade, trying to rub it off. "It's her, boss."

Boss? Xander thought, his eyes darting briefly in Randy's direction. *What kind of mistake have I made here?*

"Good," Randy said.

"Kill the hero," Duncan said, smiling so wide it showed off his sickly yellow teeth.

Randy paused, looking down the barrel of the gun at Xander. "No," he said finally. "That was part of the deal. We were given the Omega, we gotta let him go, for now." He turned to Walker. "Stay here with her."

Xander watched as Randy turned back to him, sneering contemptuously at him as he addressed the crowd.

"If any of you so much as breathe wrong for ten minutes, the girl dies. Everybody out!"

With that, all of the Tees started scrambling for the exits.

Duncan and Ian dragged Mandy, kicking, screaming, and crying for Mike's help.

Mike watched her go, blood dripping from his hands onto the floor.

"You got lucky today," Randy said, only to Xander. "Soon as that sun sets, you're fair game. I'm gonna take pleasure in killing you in your sleep."

"Right back at you," Xander said under his breath, not moving an inch for fear of Julie's life.

Randy laughed, then backed up triumphantly until he was against the doors. He turned, then left.

"Dammit."

BECOMING
CHAPTER ELEVEN

Walker glared at Xander from over the gun with a sick smile on his face. His eyes were wide and bulging with beads of sweat pouring down off his forehead every few seconds. He glanced at Julie, then turned back to Xander again.

"She's cute, man. I'd like to have a go with her, if you wouldn't mind. Wait, what am I saying?" he laughed. "Didn't she just dump you? Man you are getting shit on all over today, ain'tcha?"

"It's gonna look like sunshine and roses compared to what I'm gonna do to you," Xander said, allowing himself a smirk at the thought.

"Haven't you been paying attention?" Walker snarled. "You. Lose. Is it that hard to get through your skull? Kids today."

"Speaking of kids," Xander interjected. "Would you like to know how your daughter died?"

"Watch it!" Walker yelled.

"...Xander..." Julie moaned.

"That thing... it grabbed her right out of your back-yard. Jeez, you can't have been watching her very good, could you?"

"Shut! Up!"

"I bet that hurts. I bet you blame yourself for what he did to her, your little girl. When he bit off her arm and ate some of it. I think he had some kind of paralysis venom in his saliva or something, because she just kept on living, even after that."

"Quiet!" he yelled, putting more pressure on the trigger.

"I'm sorry, did you not know that? I knew that. I can show you the coroner's reports if you want, they're on file. I found her arm, you know."

"That's it! She dies!" screamed Walker, ready to pull the trigger.

Mike slammed Walker over the back of the head with a collapsible chair and he slammed into the floor face first.

The students broke apart like roaches when the kitchen light was turned on, scattering in all directions and making their way toward the exits.

Julie bolted straight for Xander's arms and he clasped her tightly, stroking the back of her head. For a brief, wonderful moment, he was at peace. When he opened his eyes again, they were almost black.

"Okay, guys!" he yelled, motioning to Mike and Cathy. "We gotta move fast! I didn't hear any cars so they're on foot, but they still could've gone in any direction once they got outside. We have to find her, now! Their trail gets colder every second we stand here!"

"Right." Mike nodded, as all three turned toward the

front entrance.

"I wanna help," Tommy said grimly, standing where Sud had been killed.

"Me too," Julie added, wiping the blood from her nose.

"Fine, good," Xander snarled as they walked toward the doors. "But Owchar is mine. Anyone disputes that, they become the enemy as far as I'm concerned."

"Hold it!" came an authoritative voice from behind them, grabbing Xander by the shoulder and pulling him back with amazing force.

Xander spun around and was almost blinded by the glint off the taller man's glasses.

"None of you are going after them!" O'Toole demanded. "This is a matter for the police to handle!"

Xander shot a look at Mike.

"Run!" Mike yelled, and the four of them took off out the doors.

"South on Laird!" Xander bellowed after them, praying that they'd heard it.

"Cute," O'Toole spat. He sighed, then grabbed Xander by the collar and shoved him into the wall with surprising strength, rattling the Womb within his gut.

"Argh!" Xander screamed, looking around for help to find that there was nobody there. Still, there seemed like there was. He heard something, smelled something. The Womb flared.

O'Toole sighed, turning to drag Xander into the hall.

"I never dreamed..." he mumbled, rubbing the bridge of his nose with his free hand. "...in a million years..."

"Let me go, you freak!" Xander protested, wrestling

out of his grip. "What the hell is wrong with you? Were you asleep during all of that?"

There was a sound to his right and he turned, only to find nothing there. He squinted, then shook his head and turned back to O'Toole.

"Let me go, you piece of shit!"

O'Toole lashed out, punching Xander across the face with one of his small fists.

"I am sick of your attitude, you little snot!" he screamed, kicking Xander in the gut hard enough to hurt the Womb. "You've already caused enough trouble for yourself, you fucking idiot, now what did you tell that girl?"

"What are you talking about?" Xander gasped, his mouth filling with blood.

"Does Mandy Peterson know you're the Black Womb?!" O'Toole demanded, slapping Xander across the face with his palm, sending blood against the wall.

Xander stood, stunned for a moment, then turned to face the empty corridor, then back to O'Toole.

"How did you?" he demanded, popping his claws. His eyes went from resolute to confused then back again all in the span of a few seconds. He turned around again, looking around the vacant hallway and finding nothing. "There's someone else here, isn't there?"

"Rasputin." O'Toole sighed softly, taking off his glasses and dropping them to the floor. "I believe we're past the point of discretion here, sir."

The air in front of Xander seemed to get thicker. Gradually it got worse and worse, until it was wavering like the air above hot pavement on a hot summer's day.

Out of that mist, a shape started to appear.

"I don't think that was your choice to make, Agent O'Toole."

Agent?

"I'm sorry, General, I think we've run out of options..."

General?

�↗

He watched her as she ate.

She giggled, her nose crinkling just a little as she did, in the cutest possible fashion. Just like the way that she did everything else, it was all just about as wonderfully peaceful as it could be.

The sun was shining. It was a beautiful summer day, and there were warm rays against their backs.

It all seemed familiar, so familiar... but then, this wasn't the first picnic they'd gone on.

The picnic basket was laid neatly against the red and white checkered tablecloth, spread out against the greenest grass God ever put on this earth. Ants crawled around the plates, their feelers twitching at the scent of apple pie and small cardboard boxes of cranberry juice.

"More strawberries?" Adam asked, reaching up a hand quickly to make sure that his hair was all right. It was, perfectly molded and quaffed by a half pound of extra-hold gel. He had wanted it to look perfect for her, and now was worried that it looked like a dirty blond hard hat sitting atop his scalp.

She's going to ask me why I'm all dressed up.

Eve giggled at him again, a bubbly sound, like fresh water from a spring well.

"I saw that," she taunted, scolding him playfully by waving a finger at him. "What are you all dressed up for today any-

way?"

So familiar.

"Oh, I don't know." He smiled, leaning a little closer to her. His nostrils flared to pick up more of the divine perfume that she was wearing. *"I guess I just felt the need to be half as pretty as you are all the time for a change."*

I'm so sweet.

"Aww," she cooed, tapping him playfully on the face. *"You're so sweet."*

He winked at her.

She rolled her eyes, then took one of the offered strawberries from the bowl next to his chest and pushed it past her pearly white teeth and her soft, red lips. She bit down, sucking on the tip of what remained.

He felt the hairs on the back of his neck stand on end. It always amazed him how she could be so sensual in everyday things... in everything she did, really. How she could turn him on with just a look, or the way that her raven hair fell across her breasts a certain way... or the way she could say his name when he wasn't feeling good and make all of the bad things in his life melt away.

The wind picked up and the trees all around them swayed with the breeze.

"How was the casserole?" he asked, looking down as he played with the last bit of mashed potato on his plate with the end of his plastic knife.

"It was great, baby," she assured him, motioning toward her empty plate as if to offer it as proof. She ate whatever he cooked anyway, even if it tasted like garbage, as it almost always did. *"I loved it."*

She smiled, plucking the stem off of the berry before holding *the rest out to him.*

So familiar, it seems like I've done all of this before...

He leaned in and took it into his mouth, keeping his eyes on hers the entire time, watching them light up as he kissed her fingers before he started chewing the strawberry.

"These are really fresh," she commented, picking up another and plucking the stem off of it, running the pointed side along her lips before putting it in her mouth. "Where did you get them, the deli?"

"Picked them myself. I put a few of them in the fruit salad too..."

"I noticed. It made it sweeter. Probably your best yet, hun."

Adam looked down, his cheeks turning a little red.

"No need to blush, lover," she cooed, reaching out and tilting his chin up. "This was perfect. It was just what I needed."

He smiled, blushing even more now that he knew that she had noticed it. "I know that work's been tough on you lately..."

"Work has been a nightmare." She giggled, lying back on the tablecloth. "Anderson pulled some strings and got his cousin out of the mail room (where he belongs) and up into the editing suite. I swear, there were at least fifty mistakes in last night's run, and who gets fired? Sara, that's who."

Wasn't it Lorraine?

"He really fired Lorraine?"

"No, Sara."

"Oh. That's awful."

So sure it was going to be Lorraine...

"So, his little knob cousin gets her position, and..."

"Wait, he messes up, someone else gets fired and he gets a promotion?"

"Uh-huh."

"That's insane."

"That's television, babe."

"I honestly don't know how you can handle working with those vultures. I'd have fed Anderson through the tape deck long ago."

"Simple," she said slyly, crawling over the plates to get closer to him. "I've got you to come home to, big guy."

He grinned as she leaned in to kiss him, making no motion forward as she did. Their lips met, and the sweet taste of strawberries rubbed off onto his tongue as her own came into his mouth, hot and fast, making his body tingle all over.

Suddenly, her eyes shot open and her nails dug into his side.

He opened his eyes and looked at her, saw the panic, and the fear. Their lips parted, but hers still moved trying to tell him something, trying to let him know. He drew back the hand that had been wrapped around her waist, and found that it was covered in blood. Silky, red blood dribbled down his arm to his rolled up sleeves. It soaked into the shirt he'd taken so long to pick out and expanded, soaking ever outward until it was drenched in her.

Her body slumped against the tablecloth, staining the white checkers red. The red ones remained the same, until the cloth wasn't checkered at all anymore. It was just red. Her face landed in what was left of his mashed potatoes, smearing into her hair so deep that they ingrained themselves into her scalp.

He wondered if she had even liked the potatoes, really.

He looked up.

A young man stood just on the edge of the cloth, dressed completely in black. A cigarette hung loosely between his lips as *he took small puffs, blowing them out through his nose. In his hand was a small blood-stained dagger with a handle that was etched into the shape of a dragon. He couldn't have been any older than sixteen, but his face was worn and scarred, the face of a young man who had seen too many fights in his life. His jaw was steadfast and unwavering despite the horrible thing he had just done. His eyes were black... not dark brown but black, covering his entire eye, like one great pupil.*

"What have you done?" Adam screamed, looking from his fallen lover to the madman that stood before him, cold and uncaring. There must have been some mistake. She was everything to him, all that he lived for. Rolling over and seeing her was his sole reason for opening his eyes every morning, and knowing that he could do it again the next day was his reason for closing them at night. She was his rock. His peace. His everything.

"Why would you do this to her?" he sobbed, tears streaming down his face. "What could she have possibly done?"

"She knew you," he said coldly, taking a step toward him.

Adam fell backward, turning as Xander continued to press toward him, running for the park. He passed through a knoll of trees, coming out of the other side to find himself in a graveyard. At night.

"What?" he spat, turning to see that the killer was still following him.

"You can't run," the killer taunted. "I always find you..."

He was right, Adam remembered. He does find me. He kills me.

The boy snarled, spitting his still lit smoke out of his mouth. "Black Womb sends his regards."

Adam's eyes went wide as the killer took one threatening step forward, twirling the blade between his fingers. For the first time, his stony face showed an emotion... and it could only be described as utter glee. He'd seen it on Eve's face a thousand times, and never would again.

"Why are you doing this?!" Adam screamed.

The killer said nothing, just took another calm step forward, followed by another.

Adam continued running, dodging between graves. He turned around to see how close the murderer was getting, only to find there was nobody there. Facing forward again, he came to an abrupt halt, almost falling into an open grave. He turned back around, coming face to face with Xander Drew.

"Why?" Adam begged, tears streaming down his face.

Xander actually laughed at that, driving his blade deep into Adam's gut, then pushing him into the open grave.

"Black Womb lives," he chuckled softly, spinning on his heels and stopping to light a smoke.

In his hospital bed, Genblade's heart rate slowed, slowed even more...

"He's going to go into arrest," said Porter.

"What? That's impossible!" Reilly exclaimed, rushing forward. She took one look at the charts and then backed away a step. "I'll go get the doctor!"

Xander Drew stood by the new grave of Adam Genblade, puffing away on his victory cigarette.

Suddenly, a powerful hand grabbed his heel.

He looked down, seeing Adam reaching up from out of his grave, pulling him down.

"No!" Xander screamed. "You can't beat me!"

Genblade's heart rate spiked back up to being that of a marathon runner in the bat of an eye, startling Porter as she prepared the paddles.

Adam dragged Xander down into the grave, Xander's nails forming long treads in the grass as he tried to stay above ground.

"No!!" Xander screamed as he was finally forced to let go.

Several long moments passed.

Finally, a black-clad hand slammed into the dirt above the grave, pulling himself up. Adam Genblade emerged in full costume, his black jump suit with white spikes at the joints not even tarnished by the mud and grime he had just climbed out of.

Genblade's eyes shot open.

Genblade's eyes shot open.

Porter jumped back.

"Reilly!" she tried to scream, but barely got the R sound out.

He was on his feet almost immediately, looping one arm around her and bringing his IV cord tight across her neck. The hard plastic dug deep into her throat and she coughed, her hands jolting up and grabbing at it.

He took a deep breath, in through his nose and out through his jagged, clenched teeth. Her hair smelled like mint and citrus. After over a month of unconsciousness the smell was overwhelming, as though it was the first he'd ever taken in.

There was a dry, hacking sound as Porter struggled for breath and got none.

He wrapped the ends of the cord around his fingers and pulled them tight into a fist. The cord drew tighter, wearing through the skin until it produced blood.

Her plump fingers scraped at the plastic, slipping on it over and over again as her neat, well-groomed nails failed to find a hold on its surface. The grooves of her fingertips found a hold on them once or twice, but it wasn't enough to pull it free.

She gagged again. Her eyes bulged.

"Shhh..." he soothed, leaning in until his salty lips were caressing the supple flesh of her earlobe. He smiled, giving her a small peck on her cheek. "It'll be alright."

He felt her pulse slow, and then eventually stop, her face pale white and her lips a sickly shade of blue. Her eyes were dull already as her hands fell to her sides and he let go of the cord, watching as she fell into his night stand without reacting at all.

He got up off the bed, wriggling his bare feet against the cold tile floor.

"Thanks for all your concern," he mumbled, without so much as looking at where Porter had landed. He looked down at himself and sneered at the salmon coloured paper gown he was wearing. He grabbed the stiff fabric with both hands and watched the way it bent and pushed between his fingers. He pulled it free with one quick tug, feeling the string snap against the back of his neck. It fell to the floor and he was naked in the cool, air conditioned room.

There was a needle sticking out of the crook of his left arm. His fingers grasped at it hungrily, so fast that its metal end worked itself in his veins and shredded one of the walls. He didn't care. He barely even noticed. Finally getting a good grip on it, he pulled it out, sending tiny squirts of his blood spurting against the walls.

There was an open doorway in front of him that he knew led out into the hall. He pressed his tongue along the sharpened contours of his teeth and turned instead to the door to his left.

There was a black card swipe on the wall next to it.

He reached over and grabbed the thin white strap that hung around Nurse Porter's neck and pulled, snapping the string and holding up a card key with her picture on it. It dangled in front of him and he watched it for a moment, the way it spun and played tricks with the light on its laminated surface.

He slid the key through the swipe and the light on it turned green. Pushing the door open, he entered a long hallway lined with lockers.

This room was cooler than his had been, and he felt gooseflesh ripple out all over his nude body. He stopped for a moment at a locker marked MARX in big, bold letters. He pushed in open and started pulling its contents out onto the floor. A small pair of shoes, a paperback novel, an old pair of reading glasses...

He huffed, then opened the next locker. Then the next. Then the next. Each time he reached in and grabbed a handful of its contents and pulled them out, scattering them onto the floor.

He opened his seventh and was about to reach in when he stopped and smiled.

Glimmering there in the green tinge of the fluorescent lights were the Spider-Swords.

Dual blades that had belonged to Eve when she had been alive and working for Engen. They'd been a gift from their master to her for being their greatest weapon in battle.

"It's good to be home," he sighed, picking up one of the swords.

It felt good in his hand, the weight of it. Like the citrus mint smell before, it was like holding it for the first time. It felt new and yet familiar all at once.

He looked and saw a battered black corduroy shirt on the floor and picked it up. He tilted his head to one side as if to examine it, then slid it on over his head. It was a size too small and clung to him tightly.

In his mind, it was the jumpsuit he'd last worn inside the Engen building.

He opened the locker next to his and found a ragged pair of jeans, the type that most people would have called work pants. He grabbed them and pulled them out, taking several medical textbooks with it and sending them crashing to the floor.

He smiled brazenly.

Outside Genblade's hospital room, Nurse Reilly whispered into her cell phone while poking her head around the corner, keeping an eye out for Genblade.

"Yes..." she repeated. "Yes, that's right, sir... it's finally happened."

ʌ⟨ʌ

"He did say south on Laird, right?" Cathy said between short, huffy breaths as the four of them ran down the street as fast as they could. They were exhausted enough from the fight, but the last ten minutes spent sprinting down the slow incline of the street was really starting to bog them down.

"I thought he said west on Eastman," groaned Julie, her eyes sharp and darting in all directions for any sign of her younger cousin.

"No, I said that," corrected Mike. "That's where the old Tee hideout is. If we don't catch them... we'll end up there going this way, where Laird meets Eastman."

"We're going to catch them," Tommy added, the first words he'd spoken since they'd left the school. "We have to. I won't let them hurt Mandy."

"Great. Vengeance vendettas," Cathy mumbled too low for anyone but Mike to hear. "'Cause that's exactly what a suicide mission needs."

"This isn't a suicide mission," Mike pressed, reaching out between strides and touching her shoulder. "We've made it through worse before."

"With Xander!" she snapped harshly. "Without him, we're just four kids with no knives, no guns, and no hope of beating the entire Tee gang."

Mike shot her a look to keep it down, motioning to Tommy and Julie, who were watching the roads for any sign of movement or activity.

"We're not gonna find her!" Julie wailed hopelessly, fresh blood spilling from her nose.

"Yes, we will," Tommy reiterated. "We're going to."

"We'll get there," Mike assured them. "Even without Xander here, he told us what we needed to do. We've got to stick together."

"What makes you so sure Xander's right, anyway?" Tommy said finally, looking down a side road. "I think they went this way!"

Mike turned, shooting him a look.

Tommy looked downward, dejected.

"You asked to come," Mike reminded him, addressing Julie as well. "Xander said you could. That's more than I would have done, but until he's here to tell us different, we're looking for her going south down Laird."

Cathy turned, smiling at him briefly.

Xander, she called out mentally, wishing that there were some way he could hear her; *Xander, please hurry.*

BECOMING
CHAPTER TWELVE

Xander stood wide-eyed as a middle-aged black man materialized into view. He had a goatee and some fluffy graying hair around the sides of his head, but aside from that he was completely bald. He was dressed in a black blazer and slacks with a dark gray turtleneck underneath that made him appear almost warm... but his eyes squashed that thought immediately. They were cold, and of a clear blue that was so rare for his race.

As he finished coming into view, it was like the rest of Xander's senses jump-started as well. Suddenly he was so aware of him that he didn't know how he hadn't been a few seconds ago. His cologne stank unnaturally, the cheap kind that didn't smell like any one thing but left a coppery tang in the back of your nose. The smooth fabric of his blazer rustled against the coarse fibers of his turtleneck and created a sound that seemed almost deafening compared to the silence that had been there before. His jaw clicked. And there was that hum, that dull electronic hum of white noise that always made Xander want to scream.

"General?" came a shrill voice from nowhere.

Xander looked around again, half expecting to see more invisible people coming into view.

The General brought a hand to his ear. "Reilly, I told you not to use this frequency. Switch to the private line."

There was high-pitched sound that Xander was sure only he could hear as the General kept his hand to his ear.

"I understand. This was to be expected when I showed up on the scene," he said finally, then turned back to Xander. "Now, young man, what do you have to say for yourself?"

O'Toole got a worried look on his face then, shaking his head feverishly from behind Xander.

Xander stood and stared at this new man for a moment in utter disbelief, then finally shook his head.

"Excuse me?" he said finally, furrowing his brow.

"Uh..." the General stammered, noticing O'Toole's warnings too late.

"I've had a very... very bad day." Xander informed him. "And now, we have you. Just you being here pisses me off, Mr..."

"I'm the General," he said, sticking out his chest a little with pride as he did.

"Yeah, that's not gonna happen."

"What?"

"There's no way I'm ever going to call you that with a straight look on my face, so you can drop the macho crap right... about... nnnnnow," he said sarcastically, a serious edge on his voice.

"My name is Hale," the man said, throwing Xander a

well-polished smile.

"Well then, Mr. Hale, it's been very nice meeting you," Xander said, brushing past him and flashing him his middle finger. "Please enter the nearest classroom on the left and go fuck yourself. Or O'Toole. Whatever floats your boat. I have misplaced anger to redirect."

"Womb," Hale stated, grabbing the boy by the shoulder. "Stay."

Xander eyed him for a long moment, then turned back to O'Toole, who would not meet his gaze. "Does nobody understand that I am trying to conceal a secret identity here? How do you people know who I am?"

"Xander..." O'Toole started, looking sheepish.

"Agent!" Hale snapped, as if it meant shut up. He turned back around and gave Xander that movie-star smile of his again. "Kid, I know it may not seem like it right now, but we are here to help you."

"We? Is that the royal we, or..." he sighed, looking around. "There aren't more invisible people, are there?"

Hale chuckled at that, loosening his grip on the boy. "No. No, not at all. And just because you couldn't see me doesn't mean that I was invisible. Assumptions will get you in trouble in this racket, son."

Xander paused, turning to O'Toole. "You --"

"That particular hypnotic suggestion could certainly use some work though, eh? You knew I was here from the second I walked in. Almost bumped into me a few times."

Xander squinted.

All at once, he couldn't hear anything anymore, as the flames around him started to dance and scatter away, until they went out completely. Xander looked around in confusion as a wind came from nowhere, swirling about with the force of a tornado. Zakron looked even more confused than he did, batting a debris that swirled around it as if they were its enemy. The sound like a rhythmic beating filled the air, as Xander recognized it, looking upwards just in time to see the clouds part, and a huge military helicopter descend from the sky. It hovered about twenty feet above the ground, and three cords came out of a hole in its underside. Three men, all of them wearing what resembled forest green scuba gear, slid down the ropes and landed gracefully on the ground. All three opened fire at Zakron, shooting darts into the demon's backside, and it went down in a slump. After nearly a half hour of battling it, Xander watched the thing go down with three darts.

"Obtain! Obtain!" yelled the lead scuba-man, with yellow stripes on the side of his right arm. They wore air tanks and dark goggles, showing none of their skin. They were muscular, but human in their movements and mannerisms.

"Hey!" Xander yelled, running up to the leader. "What the hell is going on here?"

"Classified, son." The commander nodded, putting an arm on Xander's shoulder. "Circe business. None of your concern. Thanks for keeping him in one place long enough for us to get a bead on him, though," he said truthfully, turning away to grab the rope and climb up as the other two loaded Zakron into the chopper.

"Hey!" Xander yelled again, grabbing the man by the arm and pulling him back down to earth. "Where do you think you're going? I've got a lot of questions, and I know you've got answers!"

"Sorry, kid." The man shrugged honestly, turning and fir-

ing a dart into Xander's gut. "Classified."

Xander fell to earth, remaining there for a moment, unable to move, just to watch the chopper pull back into the clouds, and away from sight.

"You're the Circe, aren't you?" Xander blurted.

Hale looked at him with genuine shock. "Impressive, my boy, I didn't think you-"

Xander drew back and punched Hale square in the jaw, sending him back against the lockers. "Bastards! You could have helped me, you could have saved her!"

"It was only O'Toole here!" Hale assured him. "He called us in the second it all started, but by the time I got here they'd cleared the building. I'm truly sorry, Womb."

"Stop calling me that!" Xander demanded, angered beyond imagination. "My name is Xander."

"Actually, your name is Adam. Adam Evensong. But, you knew that."

Xander stopped dead in his tracks, eyes wide.

"Been a while since you heard it though, hasn't it? Engen, Alpha Quadrant, Experimentation number 08267, if I remember correctly."

"08276, sir," O'Toole corrected, finally speaking.

"Thank you, Agent."

Xander stood, dumbfounded. "How do you people know who I am?"

Hale smiled. "We raided Engen a while back. Agent O'Toole here found the location through one of your hypnosis sessions, and he went out and got all the files pertaining to you. Truth be told, it was only then that we knew for sure that it was really you. Accounts from others indicated that it was another -"

"Harris," O'Toole interjected. "Mike Harris, another student at the school that was of the correct gender and age."

"Yes, right," Hale continued.

"Mandy..." Xander murmured.

"Yes, exactly. Smart lad."

"I have to find Mandy."

"We can't let you do that," Warren said, in his smoothest possible voice.

"Why not?" Xander demanded, spitting at Warren, his pupils getting wide.

"We have been watching you, through Agent O'Toole, for many months," Hale revealed.

"Yeah, I kinda figured that out," Xander said, rolling his eyes. "Their scent is getting cold. I have to go find..."

"You learned through Genblade that he and Engen were involved in an... in a Genetics War with us before you were called into the game, correct?"

"Yes. Fine. Whoopie. I have to go," he said quickly, attempting to rush the older man's conversation.

"We've come to recruit you for our side. Fight with us against Engen."

Xander snorted. "Check your sources pal, I destroyed Engen. Some super-spy you are."

"You destroyed Alpha Quadrant, kid," Hale said flatly.

All of the colour drained from Xander's face. "Excuse me?"

"There are more section heads in Engen than I'd care to count, each with their own lab. Alpha was just a crazed, ex-employee that got taken under a head's wing and got even more crazed. You haven't even met Engen yet, kid. And you're not ready to, not that that'll stop them."

"What are you talking about?" Xander asked, frantically. "What's going on?"

"The devil is on your doorstep, kid. That call? The reason you can't go? You're my protection. Adam Genblade just woke up, and the only person he hates more than you on this planet is me. You're not going anywhere until you've detained or destroyed that demented half-brother of yours, kid."

"I don't understand any of this," Xander said harshly, glaring at O'Toole. "I don't..."

"Kid, there isn't much time," Hale pressed. "It's time to stop playing hero, and time to start becoming one."

Xander stopped, not saying anything for a long moment as he looked at the floor.

"Otlexmndlktn," he mumbled finally.

"What was that?" Hale asked. "What did you just say?"

"O'Toole examined the location," Xander repeated, recalling what Hale had said.

"What?" Hale asked, his voice wavering.

O'Toole looked scared and wouldn't stay still. Xander noticed.

"He was at the Engen facility. The part with the computers and the caskets... where the Anti-Womb first came from." He turned, glaring evilly at Warren, who refused to meet his gaze. "You let Zakron out, didn't you, you little troll?!?" he screamed, lunging at Warren and pinning him up against the lockers, his eyes completely black now.

"I... I - "

"No more lies!" Xander demanded. "No more Circe-approved stories! I want the truth, Warren! What's really going on here?"

Warren looked past Xander at Hale, then shook his head. "As mad as you are," he said stubbornly. "You won't kill me. He will. It's not a hard choice to make."

"We'll see," Xander spat, as he let O'Toole go and turned to walk away. This time, Hale made no move to stop him.

"Genblade is coming," he said, calling after the boy.

Again, Xander merely raised his middle finger in defiance. He marched alone out into the lobby, then stopped, looking around the blood spattered room.

"Where's Walker?" he asked himself, realizing that the killer had disappeared.

BECOMING
CHAPTER THIRTEEN

Mike stopped, taking a quick look around as the rest of the group caught up. His sides ached and his lungs felt as though their strain for oxygen would soon crack his already bruised ribs. He didn't care. At that moment, a single thought coursed through his head, pumping into every crevice of his mind:

She thought I was the Womb.

Mandy Peterson had had a crush on Mike since the first day she had arrived in Coral Beach, going as far to approach him physically one of the first days that they had known each other. Since then, although her feelings for him hadn't changed, Mandy had become sweet and caring... a nice young girl, and someone that he'd come to know and care for himself, in a different way than she had initially hoped.

She'd also been through more in this life than many of the people that he knew, and for him, that was saying something. The Tees had gotten hold of her before, beating her and almost killing her. It was the Black Womb that had saved her, so of course, she had assumed that it was him. Black Womb equals White Knight in the girl's minds, he supposed.

He bent down, hands on his knees as he tried to catch his breath. The others were far behind him. How fast had he been running?

Sweat stung at his eyes as he scanned the road for any sign of movement, any hint that they'd gotten close. There was none. Coral Beach could seem like a ghost town sometimes, with enough trouble in it to keep most people off the streets. And with enough people off the street that trouble could happen. It was a vicious cycle that everyone recognized, but only a scant few were willing to step outside.

The breeze picked up and the trees next to him rustled, violently shaking as though they'd been chilled by the wind.

"This is getting useless," Tommy called out to him, limping along as he did. He'd twisted his ankle somewhere around Vietch Street and had been walking like that ever since, but he wasn't the last in line by far, so Mike had to give him credit.

Tommy was here partly for revenge, partly for another reason, Mike knew. He had feelings for Mandy, if only ones that were just beginning to spark. It must have been killing him, to first have lost his best friend to these sadists and now to be faced with the possibility of losing her.

"It's not useless," Mike returned, after a moment's lapse. He turned from the street and the trees to Tommy, and something twisted in his gut as he did so.

"Look, I'm not saying we should give up," Tommy

explained, coming up next to Mike and putting his hands on his knees to relax as well. "All I'm saying is that we try something different. Sure, I didn't hear a car either, but they could've had one waiting a block back and gone in any direction after that."

Mike nodded, his feet feeling like they were freezing to the ground. "I know," he admitted finally. "I do. I realize that what you're saying is right. But I can't think of any other options."

Tommy smiled. "How about we take the fight to Randy's doorstep?"

"What do you mean?" Julie asked, as she and Cathy came up behind them.

Tommy shot her a look. "I wasn't being cute. I mean let's go to his house and knock on his door, for Christ's sake! Come on, if you were an idiot like Owchar, wouldn't you take her to your house, thinking you'd be safe there?"

"I don't know," Cathy said, not paying attention to the three of them. "If I were Owchar, I think I'd have known that Xander would figure out a way to follow me and have left a load of Tees to dispose of us."

The trees shook again, and this time Mike jerked his head over his shoulder to see what was happening.

The face of a large man stuck out from between the branches. His eyes were wide and his face chalky white and for a moment he didn't look real, like one of the totem pole faces adventurers always seemed to stumble upon in the treasure hunt movies his father had always watched with him.

Mike shot back up as the man stepped out of the brush, revealing himself not to be made of wood but rather large, commanding muscles.

As Mike clenched his fists and set his jaw, the leaves just to the side of the pale man started to rustle as well and a second Tee came out, his red tattoo so bright and vibrant that he didn't know how he could have missed it through the green of the leaves.

Cathy backed up a pace as men seemed to come out of the trails from everywhere. There were five in total but they seemed like a hundred, like they could just keep coming out of the trees until they overwhelmed them.

"Right," Mike said as he readied himself to fight, willing his joints not to ache anymore. "Because I forgot what kind of day this was going to be."

BECOMING
CHAPTER FOURTEEN

The door to the dimly lit room squealed open slowly, projecting a beacon of light over its musty, gray floor. Randy Owchar stepped inside, taking a look around with his flashlight until he was perfectly satisfied that there was nothing waiting for him in the darkness except for what he had planned. He sneered wickedly, turning back toward the door and motioning forward.

Ian and Duncan entered, each grasping Mandy under one of her arms, and hurled her to the floor. Somewhere along the way they had stopped long enough to bind her hands behind her back and tie a blindfold around her head. Her knees and face scraped along the rocks and pebbles on the ground of the exposed basement as she rolled to a grinding halt, fresh tears soaking her mask. She sobbed violently, struggling to her knees and looking around the room for any trace of light that might shine through her mask and give her some sense of where she was.

"Please..." she pleaded, her lower lip shriveled and quivering from the tears she had shed and the tears she knew she was going to shed. "Please, I'll do anything... I won't tell anyone! Please, just don't kill me..."

Randy smiled at her, reaching deep into his pocket and pulling out Xander's dragon blade. It glinted in the damp light from the doorway, and had just a hint of blood still on it. His own blood, he thought, recalling the slash Xander had planted across his side. Slowly, he brought it down and touched the side of it, gently, to Mandy's cheek.

She froze, only the sound of her frantic breathing heard in the room as she tried to maintain her precarious balance, aware only of the cold, folded steel pressed against her face. He leaned in until he was almost touching her, running his eyes over every inch of her.

She couldn't see him, but she could feel him, and it made her shudder. More tears came.

With his free hand he reached out and pinched the fabric of her sweater, rubbing it between his thumb and forefinger.

"You dress different than you used to," he said coldly, letting go of the piece and trickling his hand over her helpless, quivering body, taking pleasure in how she trembled. He turned swiftly, seeing Duncan and Ian still standing in the doorway, watching him intently. "Close the door."

"But boss..." Ian protested, actual concern flashing in his eyes for but a brief moment.

"I said get out," Randy ordered, not even twitching in their direction this time, instead following a tear as it slowly dribbled down Mandy's smooth, freckled cheeks.

Duncan sighed, then reached out and closed the door with a loud clang, leaving the two of them alone in the dark.

She whimpered softly. Even though there had been no light before, it was more obvious now. Like how even in a blackened room you can tell when your electricity has been cut off. A sixth sense. She felt him remove the blade from the side of her face, then heard it click softly against the pavement floor as he laid it down. Feeling it was okay for her to speak again, she whimpered, managing to get out a hollow "please..."

"What?" Randy whispered, with a lover's softness.

"Please..." she said again, without hardly realizing it. "Please, I didn't tell anyone last time, I didn't. I won't tell anyone this time, I swear..."

Randy chuckled a little. "You like keeping secrets, don't you?"

"What?" she asked the darkness, her brow furrowed and confused.

"I know anyway, you don't have to hide it. Just tell me who the Womb is. I know. I also know that you know, so just tell me. I wanna hear you say it..." he spoke softly, then lashed out, smacking her across the face.

She hit the ground hard on her back, and before she could scream she felt the weight of his body crouching on her abdomen, crushing her.

"You were my first, you god damn Coral Cove slut! You! And then you betrayed me to that black freak? Tell me who he is! I want to hear you betray him, like you did to me!"

Blood seeped from her mouth as she lay, her cheek against the pavement. She was still conscious, she just didn't want to turn to face him.

"No..." she said finally, and it came out as a sob.

"Excuse me?" he spat, slamming both palms into her shoulders, bringing both her collar bones to the breaking limit at once. "I told you to do something!"

She said nothing for a moment, opened her mouth, then closed it again.

"No." she whispered, sniffling.

He sucked his lip back angrily, then picked up the blade again with a long scrape of metal that made her wince. Slowly, he scuttled downward until he was sitting on her legs, still stopping her from moving away from him. Bending down, he kissed her jeans in little, intimate pecks, making her cry even more.

"Shhh..." he cooed her, as he carefully slid the knife up between her tender stomach flesh and her sweater, then brought it up tight against the fabric. "This'll only hurt a lot."

The fabric gave way as he moved the blade upward slowly, revealing her smooth belly and naval. Her skin was so pale in the dim light that somehow found its way even here. When he was done, he pulled back the remains of her sweater, revealing her slim figure and her tiny, tea-cup sized breasts.

There were scars on them that he recognized. He'd given them to her months ago. He traced his finger along them now, feeling the raised edges of the new flesh.

He put down the knife and laid both hands on her belly and slowly moved them upward, feeling every crevice in her, remembering the way that it had felt that night not so long ago. She felt just the way that he recalled, smooth and perky against his cool touch.

She found that she had no tears left in her, only dry heaves that felt like flames burning upward from deep inside her.

"Please don't do this..." she whispered, not specifically to him.

"It's okay, Mandy," he said.

When he said her name for the first time she felt like throwing up, and had to battle the urge to do so. Her body quivered with sickness that he must have taken as encouragement, as he squeezed at her harder than before. She bit her lip, not wanting to give him the satisfaction of hearing her cries anymore.

Smiling, he bent down and brought his lips to her newly exposed flesh, soaking it with hungered saliva. She felt his breath, hard and eager. The first time a man had touched her like that she had been ten years old. She'd spent a very long time forgetting that, but now it all came rushing back and it was like he was here, too. Like they were both pawing at her at the same time.

Her mother had left her alone in the toy department at the mall again, using the Barbie's and Teddy Bears as a cheap excuse for a baby sitter while she had been going about her business. A man, someone that worked there based on her memory of what he'd been wearing, had promised her that there was a room with lots more toys, and there had been. She recalled how he had fumbled with the keys, excited. He unlocked the storage department and led her inside, where there were rows and rows of boxes. He brought her to a place far in the back, where there were lots of boxes of toys.

Randy pressed the cold steel of the knife against her

skin, feeling the gooseflesh that it created with his free hand. He laughed a little. Turning the blade so that the sharp side faced her stomach, he asked her again. "Who is he? Who is the Black Womb?"

"I won't tell you." she sobbed, her voice small and far away, but still containing so much strength.

Grunting, he drew the blade across her stomach quickly.

"Ahh!" she screamed, as she felt warmth flowed from the open wound, trickling down her body with each pump of her heart. It was a shallow cut and didn't bleed much, but it stung. She thought she was going to die.

She drove her teeth deep into her bottom lip as his mouth found the nape of her neck again. His breath stank of alcohol and cigarettes and Zesty Doritos chips. The feeling of him on her made her wish she were unconscious.

"I knew you were sweet." he said playfully, running his hands over the wound and grabbing at her stomach, the pressure making it hurt even more.

From somewhere deep inside, her body found the moisture to produce tears again.

"Let's see if you taste that sweet all over!" he yelled, excited now. He unbuttoned her pants and pulled them down quickly until they were around her ankles.

"No!" she screamed.

He reached up and grabbed her between the legs, squeezing as hard as he could.

"No!" she screamed, and continued to scream, as he used his body to force her legs apart and sunk deep inside of her, holding her squirming body down as he thrust within her again and again, faster and faster. It felt like he was ripping her apart inside, every pulse and pump full of friction and pain, like the knife that had sliced through her skin, only warmer. Sickly warm, excited. Like blood.

He started barging into her madly, losing all concept of self control or reservation as the feeling overcame him, the need to be as far and as deep in with every disgusting push as he could be.

She felt him building already, to the point when she could tell that it was going to be over very soon. There was a sticky, slapping sound as his gut smacked against her own, adhering to the blood that covered her torso and making a snapping sound when it broke free before happening again. She turned her head to the side and gazed into the darkness, away from the silhouetted movement of his body.

Mike... she thought, somewhere within the reaches of her mind. *Why aren't you saving me?*

He exploded, and she felt him fill her with rage and hatred. He pumped twice after that as his already small appendage shrunk even more, then finally withdrew.

He smiled, his breathing slowing as he pulled his jeans back up and walked toward the door. He opened it, letting Ian and Duncan in.

"All right." he said, smiling from ear to ear. "Let's see if you two can get her to talk."

Beneath her blindfold, her eyes widened as more tears came forth.

BECOMING
CHAPTER FIFTEEN

The body of George Walker hit the floor before Xander was even done asking where it had gone. He turned suddenly, spinning in a way that seemed foreign to him here. He was used to fighting in one instance, it one skin even, and being himself in another. Now, today, all that had changed. He found himself opting into a fighting stance as soon as his body finished turning, and the world of the Black Womb invaded his home, the school of Xander Drew.

Walker's half naked body slumped onto an already expanding pool of blood, his jugular slit so well that it looked like a single thin line a few inches under his chin. The rest of his body left more to be desired, bruises and slash marks tattering his flesh. There were bones and muscles showing in many areas. The man's spleen had been ripped out.

Standing over him was Adam Genblade, the very sight of which sent chills quivering down Xander's spine and goosebumps over his arms and legs. The last time he'd seen Genblade he had been lying in a hospital bed, and the doctors told him that the killer would never wake up. He should have known better. There was already blood slathered across his black shirt in several different patterns, indicating that he and his sword had already been more than a little busy. The sword itself was long a sleek, two gems on the handle forming the head and body of a spider, the handle stretching out in four different directions to make the legs. He held one in both hands, the bloodstained surface reflecting the flourescent lights into Xander's eyes and making him wince. His hair was spiked with a reddish tint, held up with dried blood that had become matted there. His thin, preened eyebrows narrowed as he looked Xander up and down with his beady black eyes, the corners of his lips curling with disgust and a disturbing smile all at once.

Xander reached for his blade, only to find that it wasn't there. His eyes darted around the floor in front of him, but to no avail. He was weaponless.

"Hey, buddy." Genblade smiled, bringing one of the blades to his lips and licking the blood from it. "How have you been?"

Xander thought about that for a moment. Open-ended questions from Adam Genblade usually ended in blood being spilt, typically his own, and the Womb wasn't even twitching, so he decided to tell the truth. "I've had better days."

"Really?" the killer asked, leaning back against the wall, as if they were two old friends just having a chat.

"Yeah, it's been kinda rough."

"Did you go into a coma?"

Xander looked from side to side, wondering if that gun was still around somewhere. "No..." he answered slowly, shaking his head from side to side and trying not to be offensive.

"Then I guess I win this one." Genblade snarled, reaching behind him and pulling out a handgun, aiming at Xander's head and firing quickly.

Xander dove forward as soon as he saw the gun. The shot traveled over his head as he rolled along the blood spattered ground, then ricocheted off the steel front entrance and broke the window that led into Schneider's office into a thousand tiny shards.

Genblade leaped to his feet, sheathing one sword so that he could carry one and the gun, pointing the barrel at Xander again.

"Because you didn't spend the last fucking month or so watching the woman you loved get murdered!"

He shot again, this time catching Xander square in the knee cap. The bone shattered, and he screamed as he fell to the floor.

"By you!" he finished, firing another shot into the fat of the same leg.

Xander screamed.

"Adam!" he bellowed, gripping the dual gunshot wounds and trying in vain to stop the flow of blood. "Adam, please! Don't do this, not now!"

"Oh, I'm sorry!" Genblade screamed, buckling over in ferocity. "When exactly would be a good time for you to be killed? Hmm? Tuesday at six good? I'll have my people call your people to confirm!"

He kicked Xander in the back brutally, with everything he had, sending him vaulting across the room and into the wall. Xander's back cracked off the brick corner, then he bounced into the pile of broken glass the first bullet had left.

Genblade walked over to him and stepped on his back, then bent over and shoved the gun barrel into the back of Xander's head.

"I like the way I play roulette better, by the way." he sneered, then pulled the trigger.

BECOMING
CHAPTER SIXTEEN

-click-

Adam's eyes filled with surprise. His face contorted in anger as he turned, heaving the gun at the wall.

"Fucking guns!" he cursed at the thing as it bounced across the floor and found its place in the corner.

"Don't blame the tools."

Genblade turned just in time to see Xander bring a long, jagged shard of glass to his wrist and rip away at the flesh and veins beneath it.

"No!" Genblade bellowed, even as blackness poured out of Xander's forearm. Instead of falling to the floor it clung to his arm, each pump bringing more and more of it up until it stretched over his arm and took on a life all its own, slithering down across his body. His head was the last to go, Xander's smile visible until the very end, until he looked like a three dimensional shadow. Three curved, red slits formed in his face, opening at once to become feline eyes and a mouth filled with dual rows of sharpened yellow teeth. He dropped the glass to the floor, where it broke again with a tiny -tink!-.

"Black Womb lives!"

The scream echoed throughout the walls of the school, coming back at Genblade from all directions.

"Argh!" he screamed, bringing his hands to his ears as the declaration attacked him. Bringing out his second sword again, he stood to face the creature in front of him, the same one that had haunted his nightmares for months on end.

"I'll kill you!" he screamed, lunging forward.

Xander leapt to the side, avoiding Adam's blades and ducking into a roll, coming up on the opposite side of the lobby with his hands clenching then extending, forcing the claws to pop from each finger to their furthest extension.

Adam turned, foam bubbling to the surface at the corners of his mouth. "You killed her! I won't let you get away from me that easily, you took her away to where I can't follow, and I'm going to destroy you for it, do you hear me?"

Xander said nothing from inside the Womb, just watched as the madman thrashed about, turning finally to face him.

All of this, all at once! he thought as he leapt away from another attack by Genblade, slashing with his claws as he did. They connected with Genblade's side, taking a large chunk of flesh with it. *What are the chances that this would happen all at once? The Tees, Circe, and now Genblade. They're all here, and I've never been so vulnerable before.*

"Genblade, listen to me!" he blurted, ducking as Genblade carried a lunge over him. He thrust his arms up, sending his claws up into Genblade's gut, then used his own momentum to fling him face first into a wall. His pointed, jagged teeth mashed into his gums, slicing them open.

"Adam, I don't want to fight you!" he pleaded, even though his words seemed to fall upon deaf ears.

"Kill you!" Genblade screamed again, driving both swords forward.

They both sunk into Xander's flesh on either side of his chest and through the other side, pinning him to the wall.

"Argh!" the Womb roared, its massive mouth opening wide and its tongue flailing about wildly. His arms tried to move but his limbs lay there, twitching and useless.

Genblade hissed, getting right up in the Xander's face until their noses touched at the tips. "Here!" he screamed, twisting both blades in opposite directions, spreading his breast plate apart.

"Fuck!" Xander screamed, to Genblade's pleasure.

"This is what it feels like to lose, Womb!" Genblade taunted, turning the blades again. "This is what it feels like to have everything you love stripped away! This is what it feels like to be dead!"

"Genblade!" Xander bellowed, forcing eye contact with his enemy. "This is not about you and me! This is bigger than the two of us, don't you get that?"

Genblade squinted, his teeth still clenched, but it was clear that he was listening. Xander had somehow managed to get his attention.

"I know I killed Eve. I could give you a million excuses- " he started, Genblade's eyes filling with rage. "-but I won't.

And I don't expect any from you for what happened to Sara. But there's someone else now, a girl that has nothing to do with either of us that I can save if you let me go, now, do you understand? We can do it together; we can make what happened right!"

The rage and the hatred slowly began to melt from Genblade's eyes, as he loosened his grip on the swords.

"Impressive." Hale said from the hall entrance behind them. "All the time I fought you, my boy, I never once thought of whispering sweet nothings in your ear."

Genblade turned to see Hale and O'Toole, along with a dozen other men in head-to-toe green jump suits and goggles that made them look like scuba divers. They were Circe men, Xander recognized them instantly.

"Tricked me!" Adam screamed, turning back and punching Xander once in the face with everything he had before ripping both of the swords out through his sides, taking a half foot of flesh with each blade. He turned to face the Circe, whose operatives raised their guns to him quickly and started pumping off rounds.

Xander hit the floor and gasped, a sound that was monstrous coming out of the Womb's mouth. There were large pieces of his chest missing under each of his arms and he wrenched in pain no other person could know while the Womb worked to repair it. It was as though something had taken two giant bites out of him and then put him away for later.

Gunfire turned the floor around him into a barrage of dust and debris. He fell to his side away from it, curling his hands up into a fetal position. His heightened senses made the crack of the guns thunderous. He thought his ears were going to start bleeding.

He opened his eyes and saw the doorway to Schneider's office was open. Cursing himself, he reached out and dug his claws deep into the tile floor and pulled himself toward it.

"Remember, men, this isn't Zakron or the Womb," Hale reminded them, reaching into his pocket and withdrawing a cigar and a pipe lighter. "If you aren't using lethal ordinance, you'd better switch now."

Several of the men switched clips, while the others made sure that Genblade got nowhere close to them, continuing to fire.

Genblade ran from one doorway to another, dodging gunfire and deflecting some off of his blades as he slowly made his way closer to Hale and O'Toole. Every time he got too close the agents would change their pattern and force him back, growling all the way.

"Still impressive." Hale smiled, motioning to him. "I don't think his downtime hurt him any. If anything, he's refreshed. Marvelous what those Engen boys could do, hmm?"

Across the room, Xander slumped to the floor, a trail of blood streaming down the wall in his wake. He was barely able to move, and most of his thoughts revolved around either thanking or encouraging his healing factor for healing head wounds first as blood hemorrhaged into his cerebellum.

"Sir," O'Toole said, stepping up next to Hale as the two of them watched Genblade flip around, avoiding the hot chunks of lead coming at him from all angles. "What about Drew?" he asked, motioning toward the boy.

"What about him?" Hale asked, turning a puffing a long trail of smoke into Warren's face. "If he can't even get up after that, he's no use to us anyway. Besides, the situation is under control."

"Hale!" Genblade yelled the word as if it were a curse, finally grabbing one the gunmen and turning him around, using his body as a human shield as bullets ripped into it, killing him. After nearly a full minute of this Genblade finally reached up and snapped his neck and tossed him to the ground. "I want you, Hale! You're just as much to blame for all of this as he is!" he yelled, pointing at Xander without even looking.

"Even more so." Hale chuckled, more to himself than anyone else, as the other operatives continued their assault on Genblade.

"Sir, are you sure it's wise to taunt him?" O'Toole asked, watching Genblade's movements intently as the blood of the downed Circe employee spilled out onto the already drenched floor.

"Oh, yes, my boy." Hale assured him, passing O'Toole a cigar. "Trust me, everything's going to plan."

BECOMING
CHAPTER SEVENTEEN

Cathy lashed out, raking her nails across the face of Elliot Matthews.

A short man with a big nose and fuzzy brown hair, Elliot was about the same height as Cathy, and the two matched each other blow for blow as he tried in vain to get his shotgun into a position where he could actually use it, but she kept him close, never allowing him to back up far enough that he could aim the massive weapon.

"Come on, big man!" she yelled at him, possibly for the tenth time, slashing at him with open palms, catching blood and flesh beneath her fingernails.

Another Tee, George McGyver, tried to grab her from behind. She shoved an elbow back, meaning to nail him in the face but connecting with his gut, turning to see a man easily twice her size with white hair and a broad chest clutching his stomach as he toppled over in pain.

Tommy was being held on from behind by Mark Clevet, a scrawny youth with a buzz cut and scruff to match it, another Tee trying to look like their leader, Roulette.

"What's the matter?" Mark bellowed into Tommy's ear as Justin Langley, a kid that looked like he came straight out of that painting *The Scream* punched him as hard as he could first to the face and then to the upper torso. "Can't you take a little fun?"

Tommy's head wobbled around like a bobble head, and he began to lose consciousness.

ᚕ

Mike threw Dwayne Piercey to the ground for the third time, mashing his face into snow which was now turning red. Mike was bleeding from slash marks that ornamented his arms and chest, but he found that they did not bother him too much, as the satisfaction of slamming his foot into the back of Dwayne's head took over. When he relinquished, he realized that Dwayne was unconscious and bleeding from both a split in the roof of his mouth and a broken nose. He smiled, then turned his attention toward Ryan Crocker, a bald man wearing a sweater who was aiming a gun across the fight at Cathy.

"Come on, guys!" he yelled in encouragement. "You can do this!"

ᚕ

Sven Douglas slammed his fist into Julie's face, smiling with those idiotic buck teeth as he did so, her blood covering his knuckles. He laughed a little, a disgusting sound, as she raised her arms in a weak attempt to block his attack. He took the opportunity to punch her in the gut, hard, knocking the wind out of her as she fell backward into the snow.

He stepped closer.

"Now, bitch!" he laughed, backhanding her across the face and then reaching for his gun.

Her head jerked to the side, traveling with his blow. As it did she caught a glimpse of Tommy, blood streaming from his nose and mouth as Langley continued to slam into him. Turning back, she brought back a leg and kicked him as hard as she could, squatting his finger and making him retract the hand that was going for his weapon.

"Mike!" she screamed, cocking her chin at Tommy.

๙๙

Mike turned to her, laying a finishing blow on Crocker and sending him down for the count, then followed her gaze to where Tommy stood. Thinking quickly, he reached down and scooped up a handful of snow, packed it as tightly as he could, and ran toward the two Tees. He stopped only for a moment, letting the fist-sized ball of ice sail though the air as fast as he could. It slammed into the back of Langley's head with an explosion of white. When the large man turned, he had just enough time to see Mike's fist coming toward his face.

"Hey!" Clevet yelled, loosening his grip on Tommy just long enough. Tommy shot back an elbow, knocking the wind out of his captor, turning to plant a fist clear across his face.

"Hey yourself." he grumbled, kicking the Tee in the head.

∧‹∧

Cathy grabbed Elliot by the hair and slammed him into a tree, breaking the young man's nose and sending him to the snow, out cold.

"Hey!" she squealed happily. "I got one!"

Just as she spoke George got up again and launched himself into her, slamming her to the ground and pinning her there.

"Slut!" he yelled, drawing back and punching her in the jaw. "You've fucked everything up! I'll teach you some manners!"

He punched her in the chest.

She coughed hard, trying to catch her breath and get him off of her at the same time, succeeding with neither.

"Grendel, please..." she pleaded. He already had her shirt off, and now he had her jeans unbuttoned. "Please, just stop."

George grabbed at Cathy and punched her across the face, smiling devilishly as he did.

The tears ran down her soft, freckled cheeks. She sobbed. He stopped for a moment and looked up at her, then starting to pull down her jeans.

She brought her knee up fast, catching George in the groin but seeing Grendel.

He stumbled backward, clutching his privates with both hands.

"You fucking bitch..." he whined, his eyes bulging with pain.

Tight lipped, she got up. She drew back and nailed him in the jaw as hard as she could.

"You'd better believe it," she spat down at him.

ﻉﻉﻉ

Sven had managed to get his handgun out, and Julie was now wrestling with him for control of it, the both of them rolling around in the snow, biting and punching at one another for control over the weapon.

ﻉﻉﻉ

Tommy laid in a final punch to Steve, sending him down for the count, then turned to help Mike with Langley, who currently had Mike held by the throat.

BANG!

All heads turned, wondering where the shot had come from.

Sven turned, the gun now visible in his hand, as well as the fountain of blood streaming out of the gaping maw in Julie's chest.

"No!" Tommy screamed.

Mike slammed Langley into the frozen ground and they both ran toward her. Cathy turned the corner and saw what was happening, and all three of them bolted toward Sven, who dropped the gun in fright as both men pounced on him. Cathy went to Julie's side.

"Julie!" Cathy screamed, pulling the girl's hair out of her face and being very careful not to touch the wound. "Julie, are you all right?"

"Don't..." she tried to say, as blood gurgled up from her throat. "Don't stop. You have to find her."

"We will. And we'll save you, too. We will." she assured her, taking the girl's hand and rubbing it. She turned to Mike and Tommy, who were both wailing on Sven's face. "Will you two stop fucking around over there and come help me?"

Tommy took the words to heart immediately, bolting toward Julie. Mike lay one final blow into Sven, making sure he was down.

"Oh my God." Tommy gasped, his hands instantly covered in red liquid. "There's blood everywhere."

"We have to get her to a hospital." Mike said firmly.

"No..." Julie protested, losing consciousness.

"She wants us to find Mandy." Cathy tisked. "What are the chances of that now, anyway?"

Tommy grunted. "Where's the hospital?"

Mike stopped, looking around for a moment. "Three blocks down, one over... why?"

"I'll take her, you guys go on ahead!"

Mike stopped, considering this for a moment. "Where did you say Randy lived?"

"What?" Cathy exclaimed, as Mike helped Julie onto Tommy's back.

"Fifty-six Roberto," Tommy said, grunting with the added weight. "It's the white one."

"Got it," Mike said, putting a hand on Tommy's shoulder and giving it a squeeze.

Tommy nodded, then took off with Julie, as gently as possible.

"This is insanity!" Cathy screamed, running her blood soaked fingers through her hair. "There's no way that he's going to make it in time!"

"Yes, they will!" Mike said loudly, without yelling, as though trying to convince himself. "Now come on. I've got more scum-punching in me today."

BECOMING
CHAPTER EIGHTEEN

Genblade grabbed a Circe agent and sliced him across the gut with his sword, spilling blood and bladder onto the floor as he did so.

"General, this is insanity!" O'Toole yelled.

Many of the men dropped their ammo-less weapons and picked up tasers and knives from their belts, slashing them about, the tasers crackling with energy.

"Genblade is going to kill us all, do you realize that?"

Hale just smiled, watching the fight with a childish glee.

O'Toole grunted, turning away from his commanding officer and toward the battle, running between wet works agents over to where the Black Womb lay bleeding.

"Drew!" he yelled, grabbing the boy by the shoulders and shaking him violently. "Drew, are you okay?"

The Womb reacted quickly, reaching up and grabbing Warren by the wrists and digging his claws in deep.

"Better, now that you're here," he said sharply, his monstrous mouth contorting into a sick smile. He spun

Warren around, slamming him into the wall where he had been. "Now, you're gonna tell me what's going on here, and you're going to be as quick as possible about it, or I'm gonna show you what you've been playing at for months!"

"Okay!" Warren yelled, squirming as blood trickled down him arm.

There was a frenzied scream in the background as Genblade took out another operative, his sword biting at the main vein of the man's leg. Arterial blood splashed up at Genblade, soaking the lower half of his face and mouth.

"Circe and Engen were rivals, right? Have been for decades. It started with them trying to outbid each other for government rights to the programs like the one that created you, but when the U.S. and Canada lost interest, it just turned into a Cold War!"

"Why me? Why am I a part of this?" he demanded, grabbing Warren by the collar and shaking him.

"Engen had Genblade and Eve and Zero and all the rest... even the Anti-Womb! And this had been going on for years, with the Circe scientists coming up with squat to compete. We even started hiring out of other labs making genetic freaks, just to defend ourselves. So, when we heard that Alpha had tried to tap you... we were as shocked as you were. Hale sent me here, after Phillips got canned. Sent me to find out which one of you kids was the Womb."

"And Zakron?" the Womb bellowed, shaking the frightened man again. "Why would you let Engen's deadliest weapon out?"

"To draw you out!" Warren screamed, clutching at his

throat and trying to get more air. His lips began to turn a pale blue, becoming paler every time Xander shook him.

"What do you mean 'draw me out'?" the Womb demanded, loosening his grip slightly.

"I was sure it was you, from the moment I laid eyes on you." Warren blurted, gasping for air. "But Hale needed convincing. Needed to see you transform. We'd been wrong too many times before. Xander, there's something you have to know..."

"Obtain! Obtain!" yelled the lead scuba-man, with yellow stripes on the side of his right arm. They wore air tanks and dark goggles, showing none of their skin. They were muscular, but human in their movements and mannerisms.

"Hey!" Xander yelled, running up to the leader, "What the hell is going on here?"

"Classified, son." the commander nodded, putting an arm on Xander's shoulder, "Circe business. None of your concern. Thanks for keeping him in one place long enough for us to get a bead on him, though." he said truthfully, turning away to grab the rope and climb up as the other two loaded Zakron into the chopper.

"Hey!" Drew yelled again, grabbing the man by the arm and pulling him back down to earth, "Where do you think you're going? I've got a lot of questions, and I know you've got answers!"

"Sorry, kid." the man shrugged honestly, turning and firing a dart into Xander's gut, "Classified."

Xander fell to earth, remaining there for a moment, unable to move, just to watch the chopper pull back into the clouds, and away from sight.

Xander froze immediately, raising his hands in the air. He might... might be able to survive a blast at this range, depending on where it hit, but there was no guarantee that nobody else would get hit either.

"Turn around," Randy ordered.

Again, Xander complied, biting his lip about the fact that he knew he could take down that son of a bitch child-killer in ten seconds flat.

"Well, well, well," Randy smiled, shaking his head at Xander. He lowered his voice considerably, so that only he and Xander could hear. "If it isn't the Black Womb."

"Kill the hero," Duncan said, smiling so wide it showed off his sickly yellow teeth.

Randy paused, looking down the barrel of the gun at Xander. "No," he said finally. "That was part of the deal. We were given the Omega, we gotta let him go, for now." He turned to Walker. "Stay here with her."

Xander watched as Randy turned back to him, sneering contemptuously at him as he addressed the crowd.

"If any of you so much as breathe wrong for ten minutes, the girl dies. Everybody out!"

Xander turned and slashed his claws across Warren's face, then allowed him to topple to the floor.

"Bastard!" he screamed, spitting out the last of the blood in his mouth. "You did this, didn't you? You fucking fed Mandy to the Tees just to draw me the fuck out, you sick bastard!"

"Xander," O'Toole pleaded, scrambling to his feet. "If you'll just give me a moment to explain..."

Xander drew back and punched Warren in the face, sending him stumbling backward.

He fell into the waiting arms of Adam Genblade, either of his armpits wedged in the crooks of the killer's arms.

"Well well," Genblade chuckled, bringing the blade to Warren's throat. "Special Delivery from my good friend the Black Womb. And it's not even my birthday."

"Let him go." Xander ordered calmly, standing with his back arched. "He's mine."

"Didn't know you had a new boyfriend..." Genblade teased. When it got no response he continued unabated. "I'll tell you what. You wanted to go rescue the damsel? Fine. But only if you leave me here. I'm giving you and yours this one chance, Xander. You really should take it."

Xander clenched his teeth and balling his hands into fists.

"Do what you will," he said, then turned toward the doors.

"Ha!" Genblade yelled victoriously, then sliced through the tender flesh of Warren O'Toole's neck.

Blood squirting in all directions, lapping out onto the floor like red raspberry punch from the fountains that the school rented year after year for the prom. O'Toole did not speak or gasp or even barely move at all. His eyes were wide and white almost at once, and his cheeks were flushed. He did not reach for his throat or try to stop the flow the way people always did in the movies. Instead he stood there, propped by his killer's steady hand, and spewed thick blood the consistency of jelly out onto the last good shirt he would ever wear. His head toppled back and widened the slit, revealing the pink meat of his scrawny neck muscles as they wrapped around the barest hint of an adam's apple, clutching at it and making sick slurping noises as it sputtered and spat and spewed more blood out.

Genblade laughed hysterically, turned toward the three remaining Circe Operatives and Hale, and dropped the body to his feet in a bloody slump. "Kids these days, eh?"

Hale's eyes finally opened wide with fear as he watched Xander exit the room.

"Womb..." he said, softly at first, as the boy closed the doors behind him. "Womb! Don't do this, Womb!"

One of the Circe operatives stepped forward, holding his gun in both hands and intending to use it. Genblade had never had qualms about killing, especially not people in this line of work, but the full-body suits that they wore made it even easier. They all looked the same, their faces completely covered. It was like they weren't even real. This one was scrawnier than the rest. His muscles were toned, but there was no gristle on them. Genblade ventured that the man beneath the wetsuit was no more than twenty-five.

He stabbed the man in the chest, then swung him around on the tip of the blade and forced him to the floor, pinning him there.

There were screams, magnificent ones, as the man tried to move but couldn't.

Genblade kicked at the his head with his steel-toed boots, over and over again, his leg moving so fast that it was a blur. The screams had stopped, but the sounds that had replaced them were just as wretched. Each kick was accompanied by a wet crackling sound, like crushing a ripe bell pepper between your hands. Every so often there was a loud snap, but after a few kicks the sounds became slushier, like tossing a damp sponge into a dirty bucket.

The man's mask had filled up with blood. His eyespieces, like a diver's, were filled with the dark red liquid. It sloshed about them like water in a half-filled glass, and was the only outward indication from the neck up that there was even anything wrong with the man.

Genblade propped his foot against the man's shoulder for support, then pulled the blade from his chest with both hands the way Arthur had pulled Excalibur from the stone.

"Womb!" Hale called again, backing up one pace, then another. "For god's sakes, Womb! You can't leave us in here!"

Genblade grabbed another scuba-man and shoved his face into a wall. The impact sent blood spatter all the way up to the ceiling. He shoved the third and final man to the floor, now only interested in clearing the path between himself and Hale, stomping it methodically as Hale continued to back up.

"Womb!" Hale screamed, even as Genblade grabbed him, drew back the Spider-Sword, and aimed for the center of his torso.

ʎ⟨ʎ

Outside, Xander paused as he heard Hale's screams. He turned to look back at the school, then forward at the road ahead.

BECOMING
CHAPTER NINETEEN

"Womb!" Hale shouted as Genblade drove the blade forward. It sliced clean through him, spewing blood out through the treads of the sword.

Genblade withdrew and let Hale fall to the ground, still alive. Blood was coming out of the gaping hole in the man's chest. It was so dark and bubbled out so furiously that it looked like oil escaping from a sprung vein, soaking through his clothes and into his skin. He was bleeding to death, and quickly.

"Isn't this interesting?" Genblade sneered, watching the life pump out of Hale's veins. He danced around Hale in a small circle, then leaned down to grin right in his face. "After all this time it's you that's going to fall, not me. Not like you always said. And I'm not even going to give you a decent death, you see that? You're going to die bleeding and mewing like a stuck cat and I'm going to watch. It's over now, do you get that? The Circe is done, do you hear me? Are we clear?"

"Crystal."

Genblade turned just in time to see Xander's claws coming toward his face.

They connected, all four of them ripping a different line through Genblade's skin, like tiny ditches dug for blood to flow through.

"Argh!" Genblade screamed, his head flying forward into his palm as his face burned. "Can't I ever be rid of you?"

The second Spider-Sword lay dormant in its holster against Genblade's back, the handle pointing toward Xander. He grabbed it and spun it around in his fingers as though it belonged there, the light gleaming off of it onto the walls.

"Apparently not," he returned, holding the blade at the ready. "No matter how much we both may want it."

He lashed out with the sword, bringing it down toward Genblade's downed head.

Genblade rose quickly, bringing his arm up and bending it until his blade ran parallel to it and blocked the path of the attack.

The blades met only briefly but made a spark so bright that it was like a camera flash had gone off between them.

Genblade spun on his heels and jabbed the blade out from his hip in a short, savage little thrust.

It had almost connected to Xander's hip when he brought his blade around and batted it away clumsily, then spun it back around to hold it with both hands. The momentum took Genblade's sword with it, sliding the blades together and making sparks fly as the blades locked into a stalemate and the both of them came nose to nose.

"How did this happen? How are you so deep into every part of my life?" Genblade spat, swiftly raising a knee and kicking Xander in the gut, forcing him back a pace. He slashed across Xander's face, causing the blackness to tendril off of the pink flesh underneath in long, swirling motions for a moment, revealing the bruised, scarred facial tissue beneath it.

"Just lucky I guess," he offered, his face slamming into lockers as he attempted to roll with the blow in the enclosed space. He felt a long, jagged tooth break off and travel down his throat, ripping everything it touched along the way.

"Shut up!" Genblade demanded, slashing forward with the blade again, ripping through Xander's chest. "Don't you get it? This is the day when you will finally fall!" He brought the blade up high, holding it with both hands, ready to slice Xander right down the middle.

Genblade brought the blade down, only to have the Womb catch it at the last possible second with his free hand. He gripped it tightly, drawing dark blood from a straight line across his fingertips.

"Maybe," he agreed, his voice gruff and painful to hear. "But that doesn't mean it'll be you!"

He pushed forward, forcing the sharp handle of the blade into Genblade's face.

"In case you haven't noticed, there are plenty of people around just waiting to do that!"

Genblade tumbled backward, growling deep within his throat. He raised his sword again and attacked blindly, full of rage. He slashed his sword again and again at the air, sometimes near Xander and sometimes not, raked grunts emerging from his throat with every push. He'd lost all the finesse he'd had a moment ago, and yet was still forcing Xander back. Glaring banefully, he locked eyes with Xander once more and drove his sword forward.

Xander dodged to the left to be free of it, springing up on his heels to get him further away.

In the distance, he heard sirens. An ambulance, and a police cruiser several blocks down.

"When I'm done with you, I'm going to find the Tees like you were talking about doing." Genblade hissed, holding his sword at the ready as he took step after step toward Xander.

Xander glanced over his shoulder with those deep, red eyes of his taking in everything, backing up again and trying to stay out of arm's reach.

Genblade slashed forward, taking a chunk out of Xander's leg.

"I'm going to kill them all and suck the marrow from their bones. Then if they haven't killed that little bitch you were talking about," he snarled, jumping forward a pace, connecting the blade with Xander's mid-section and narrowly missing his diaphragm. "I'll take those hollowed out bones and use them on her. She'll think those little two-pump chumps were nothing by the time I'm through with her. Oh, the blood'll taste so good..."

Xander sprung to its feet and lunged.

Genblade caught him by the throat and slammed him into the stone wall, driving his sword deep into his gut. The blade penetrated just above his naval. He was careful not to hit the Womb organ. He wanted this to last as long as possible.

"You won't touch her." Xander demanded, through pursed, dry lips.

Genblade chuckled. "That's the funny thing. I wouldn't have, if you'd only let me kill Hale in peace.. You see? You've doomed them all with your hero schick, get it?"

He twisted the blade, taking perverse pleasure in the moist, warm sound it made.

"I wonder if I can make Cathy make sounds like that, Xander?" he poised, smiling, watching Xander's eyes grow. "I never did thank her for that time she flirted with me in the visitors booth. I warned her what I was going to do. Bitches never learn, do they?"

He laughed, then got a thoughtful look on his face as he twisted the blade a full three-hundred and sixty degrees.

"Come to think of it, I learned that from another girl. Now who was that?" he asked. "Oh, yeah: Sara."

"Argh!" he yelled as both Xander and the Black Womb, forcing both his arms forward as he broke free of the sword's grip, ripping and rendering him own flesh to do so. Deep inside him, the Womb pumped ferocity through him, fueled by Genblade's words and the certainty that they were true. The organ stopped only for a moment, then began pumping to a different beat, quicker, readier.

All at once, Xander's eyes changed from red to aqua, a kind of blue-green shade that most people identified with the sea, but people who knew Xander Drew identified with merciless death, as his consciousness was forced away into a corner where it could not be heard, and only one thing ruled the Black Womb's body : itself.

All of its wounds healed over, all of its scars repaired

themselves as the fight started over again for the creature, rejuvenating it as it looked upon its enemy with new eyes.

"BLACK WOMB LIVES!"

"That's more like it!" Genblade smiled, slashing his blade forward into the Womb's gut, spilling blackness everywhere.

The Womb barked, then slashed back. Its claws seemed longer now, and red blood dripped from their roots as they extended even further.

"That's it!" he shouted happily. "That's the man I've been waiting four months to see! Now show me the face you used when you killed my wife, you fucker!" he demanded, slicing long cuts into the Womb. He withdrew the blade, ready to stab it forward again, when the Womb caught it.

The creature held it for a long moment, squeezing with all its might.

"No..." it said, in Xander's voice. Suddenly, the creature's eyes turned red again.

"What..." Genblade gasped in disbelief.

The Womb broke the sword, shattering it into hundreds of tiny shards. They scattered to the floor like organ-pipes ripped from their moldings, each one making a loud clang as it hit the tile floor. Each sound was different from the last, echoing off the walls and becoming louder until a cacophony of cymbals assaulted Genblade's ears.

"I'm not going to give you the satisfaction."

"Argh!" Genblade yelled, leaping forward.

Xander swirled around the piece of sword that he still held in his hand, digging it deep into the side of Genblade's neck, then letting it go.

Genblade just stood there for a moment, blood oozing out of the open wound, his neck hanging half open, then he slumped to the floor just as Xander heard the paramedics pull into the driveway.

"There."

Inside Xander, a battle was still being fought as the True Womb tried to take over. "Ugh." he grunted, holding his gut.

"Hale..." he called, turning around. "Hale, help me."

When he looked, the man called Hale was nowhere in sight. There wasn't even any blood where he had been curled on the floor after Genblade had stabbed him in the chest.

Xander coughed up blood as the beast pounded through the doors, taking over again, turning his eyes a sickly green.

"BLACK WOMB LIVES!"

BECOMING
CHAPTER TWENTY

The front door to fifty-six Roberto Drive burst open, shattering the knob as Mike and Cathy stepped inside.

The house was dark despite the fact that all its lights were on, the beam from each fixture seeming to only make it a few feet. It was a long bungalow of the type that had gone out of style in the early eighties, with white vinyl siding that was burnt and charred on at one corner.

The inside seemed to be a trap for light. The carpet was the mixed fibre shade of a mongrel cat's fur or vomit after a day of eclectic tastes, with no discernible pattern or style. The result was uneven, but dominantly greenish-gray. It exuded shadows.

Walls that had started off eggshell had been stained a putrid yellow by nicotine.

The both of them stepped past the small inlet which was the porch (had to, in fact, so that they could both stand side by side) and into the hall. To one side of them was a quaint living room, and to the other was a mostly vacant dining room. Ahead was a small table with an old rotary phone on it, and beyond that was a hall that led into the bathroom. The furniture was passable in this light, but under brighter scrutiny Cathy thought that there would be chips and dings in them. They'd likely been purchased at the flea market that was held down by the Super Eight once a month.

She decided at once that this was a man's apartment. Everything was utilitarian. Nothing for comfort or to add warmth.

"Hello?" Cathy called out, cupping her hands over her mouth. "Is there anybody in here?"

"Cheap locks." Mike mumbled, closing the busted door frame.

"Hello?"

A fat head appeared from around the corner of the washroom, sticking out from the frame a little higher than they would have expected and looking like it was just floating there. It was completely hairless, even devoid of eyebrows. There were traces of white residue around his ears and a towel coloured the same wrapped tightly around the rolls of his neck. The flesh protruded around it above and below, as though it were trying to suck the towel in and swallow it.

There were boils behind the man's ears, but the head was otherwise smooth.

"Oh!" The man smiled an embarrassed little smile as we walked out to greet them. "I'm sorry, I didn't hear you come in. I was getting ready to take a shower."

"Okay." Mike said, raising an eyebrow. He looked at the man for a long moment, narrowing his eyes. He was shirtless with globs of condensation and sweat glistening underneath his nipples. There was a tuft of fuzz in the center of his chest that represented the only hair Mike could see, hovering between the two ends of the towel as though it were a part of it. And while his chest and arms jiggled with fat, his stomach was flat and toned as it went down into the denim of his jeans. He looked like he had been in shape, once, and was now slowly trying to be again. "We're looking for Randy, have you seen him?"

The man furrowed his brow, thinking.

"No... not for a few months." his expression changed then, from confused to concerned. "Why? Have you seen him? Is he okay? God, I haven't even heard from him since that day at school. I can't believe that that was my Randy..."

"You're his father?" Cathy asked, looking the man up and down.

Mike took a step to the left as Cathy's shoulder bumped into his in the narrow space. The light from the living room's bay window now played tricks with the water on the man's shoulder, making it glimmer. He didn't have any tan lines, Mike noted. The hairless look was not a new one for him. The man had almost the same pale fleshy tone to himself all over, actually. The only discoloured thing on his body was his ring finger, the flesh there much sallower than the rest in a smooth line.

"Yes." the man answered, offended by the question visibly.

"I'm sorry." Cathy replied honestly. "You just don't look old enough to have a fifteen year old son."

"I'm not." he sighed, chuckling a little. "My names Terrence. Terrence Owchar, by the way." His voice was deep and booming, but somehow very kind at the same time.

Mike took a slight step to the left again. Each time he did his perspective on the man changed slightly, showing a different part of him or the house around him. He could see the darkened oblongs of several doorways in the hall behind him now, where Terrence and Randy's bedrooms not doubt where. There was a table against the wall in between them that had a few crisp bills on it near the base of a picture frame that looked to be at least fifty years old. There was a vase next to it, glimmering blue with pascal flower print. At the end of the hall in the bathroom, he could see the mirror and the sink beneath it now. It was covered with steam, and he didn't know how he'd missed when they'd come in.

"So, you haven't seen Randy?" Cathy asked again, shaking her head and smiling.

Terrence shifted a little to the right. "No, of course not. Not since the police have been looking for him. I don't put up with those shannanighans in my house."

Mike shifted a little, tilting his head down. There was a shaving brush leaned against the faucet with bits of foam still stuck to its smooth brown bristles. Beside it was a small square made of black plastic, attached to a cover of clear plastic by a winch. It was open against the porcelain with a small wedge of sponge resting in it. The wedge was smeared and splotched with red and white.

"What did you say your names were?" Terrence asked.

"Oh!" Cathy smiled. "I'm Cathy Kennessy, and this is Mike Harris. We were... um, friends of Randy's before, you know..."

"I see." Terrance said, nodding. "You don't think he did it, do you?"

"I... can't say." Cathy said. "But if he did, I'm sure it's just because of the awful crowd he managed to get mixed up in."

"Yes..." Terrance nodded, shifting his obese body to the right again. "How do you suppose he got hooked up with those hooligans?"

"He's a legacy." Mike mumbled, turning from the bathroom and back to Terrance.

"Excuse me?"

"I always wondered what it stood for... never once occurred to me it was something so simple as the first letter of someone's name." Mike said, laughing humorlessly to himself.

"What are you talking about?"

Mike motioned toward the bathroom behind Terrence. "The makeup back there."

Terrence turned briefly to look where Mike was pointing, but didn't really have to. He knew exactly what the young man was talking about. When he turned back to them his eyes had shrunk into tiny black dots in the middle of his head. His brow was pushed forward like a caveman's, making a thick dark line across that shadows of his face, bisected by his thick Irish nose.

"You know now that I see it, I don't know how I didn't before --"

"I really think you'd better --"

"Roulette."

Terrence shot forward at Mike, crossing the distance

between them in one great stride. He wrapped his plump fingers around the boy's neck and squeezed, forcing him against the wall that divided the living room from the hall.

Cathy screamed.

Mike reached up and tried to pull Terrence's fingers away. The flesh of his clubbed digits felt smooth and greasy, like plump Polish sausages. They were impossibly hard to get a grasp on, and Mike found his hands sliding fruitlessly around Terrence's bare arms rather than coming up with a good hold.

His face had turned pink immediately. Now it was a bright shade of red.

He made a sickly gasping sound as his mouth reached for air and found none, his windpipe held closed by Terrence's massive hands.

Cathy screamed again, louder than before.

Terrence's eyes were bulging now, his pupils so small and furious that they almost disappeared into the white marble of his sclera. His mouth had been contorted into a lemniscate that showed off all his teeth when he's started, but now was bent into a malicious smile. Spit frothed at the edges of his mouth and fell onto Mike's shirt as he shook the boy, pressing harder on his neck.

Mike kicked out, slamming twice into Terrence's stomach. It was like kicking concrete. A third kick connected with his groin. In registered a reaction, though not much of one.

Cathy screamed a third time.

"Jesus, what does it take for that bitch to shut up?" Terrence bellowed, turning to look over his shoulder.

Cathy smashed the blue vase into his face. The clay broke into hundreds of sharp little pieces that slashed at his cheeks as he fell over, slamming his head against the wall and releasing his grip on Mike. Ashes from inside the vase toppled down over him in weighty clumps, finding their way into his eyes and mouth. They stuck to his sweaty, moist skin even as the impact of his fall shook much of it off.

Mike looked at her as he gasped for air on his knees. "Thanks." he nodded, swallowing hard. It burned when he did.

"Not a problem." she frowned, dropping what remained of the urn to the floor. The ashes turned the multicoloured carpet a sickly but uniform gray.

From the floor, Terrence moaned. His hand was moving.

"What do we do about him?" Cathy asked, taking a step back.

Mike got to his feet, still caressing his neck with one hand. It still had the shape of Terrence's fat fingers pressed into them. He walked over to the puke green rotary phone that stood on the table and placed his hand on its receiver.

He stood like that for a moment without moving.

"What?" Cathy asked, taking another big step away from Terrence. "What is it?"

Mike did not respond. There was a drawer in the table that had been left ajar. Something twinkled in it now, the way the light had twinkled off the sweat on Terrence's shoulders a few minutes before.

Slowly, he took his hand off the receiver and picked

up the shimmering object.

They were brass knuckles.

He turned a looked at Terrence's hand. The sallow flesh of the ring finger he'd seem before was still there, but now he saw what he'd missed the first time: all the fingers on that hand had sallow rings around them, forming a straight line across his knuckles.

"Are those?" Cathy asked, next to him now and glaring down at the brass in his hand.

"Yes." he replied, before she could even finish the question.

He finally picked up the telephone receiver, and handed it to Cathy.

With a vacant face and a throbbing neckline, he closed the distance between himself and Terrence again until he stood over the larger man. He slid the brass down over his fingers until it made a line roughly adjacent to where the line had been of Terrence's.

Cathy dialed the police, a number she knew by heart by now.

They would be a long time coming she knew, with everything that had happened at the school.

Mike drew his fist back as far as he could, then brought it down.

〳〵

Ian zipped up his fly, spitting down upon the beaten, bleeding body of Mandy Peterson.

"Everybody given her all they can?' Duncan asked, kicking her in the ribs as he spoke.

She didn't make a sound. She barely moved. Barely

breathed. Her skull had been cracked open by one of them, matting her hair in blood. The vessels in her right eye had all popped, turning the white red and giving her a demonic appearance. Two of her teeth were missing, and another was chipped. Her face stung as fluids not her own seeped down it. Her nose had been broken, the roof of her jaw cracked.

They had sliced at her breasts with broken bottles and poured alcohol onto them, making them burn and ache. One of them had broken her legs while he had ridden her, and her left wrist was sprained. Blood and semen seeped slowly from her genitals as she stared wide-eyed into the darkness, her mind devoid of all thought, body broken and not her own anymore.

"Two's my limit." Randy admitted, sighing.

"Me too." Ian smiled, purposely stepping on her foot with all his weight as he stepped over her. He joined the others, then turned to watch her. "Should we let her heal up until we're ready to go, or -"

"Naw." Duncan snarled, taking out his gun. "She don't look half as pretty anymore. I think we're done with her, boys."

He pulled back the hammer on the gun, aiming it at her swollen, bruised face. "Bye bye. I'd love to say some kind, parting words, girl... but you weren't that good."

He paused.

"Come on, guys." he smirked, still looking down the barrel of the gun. "That was funny!"

He turned toward them, only to find that they were no longer paying any attention to him. They were facing the open doorway where the Black Womb stood, its eyes glowing blue-green against its silhouette, claws at the ready, hunched over and breathing so hard that it echoed off the unseen walls of the warehouse.

"Oh my god." Randy whispered, reaching to his pocket and getting out his taser. "Shoot it! Fast!"

Duncan turned his gun and opened fire on the Womb. The bullet hit its mark, sinking into its flesh where its human heart was. The creature did not flinch, did not move for a long moment, and even then, it only took a single step forward.

"Shit!" Ian cursed, fumbling about in the darkness for his gun. "Where the fuck did I fling it to? Stupid bitch made me friggin' forget, and now I..."

He looked up.

At first he saw nothing, only darkness. Then Duncan fired another shot, one that actually hit the darkness in front of him and made it bleed shadows. He tilted his head further up as the Womb knelt down until they were at eye-level. It hissed, long and snake-like, bending over quickly to bite Ian's throat with all eighty-four of its teeth and ripping it out, leaping onto him as he tried to scream but couldn't, its hind legs coming up and ripping at his chest with feet claws like a cat while its talons reached around to the rapist's back and ripped off two gigantic strips of flesh. The creature got up, covered in blood from the waist down, bent over and ate the two pieces of flesh in one bite.

Duncan fired again, this time hitting it between the eyes to no effect. The creature took a menacing step forward. Duncan fired again, hitting its mark in the central plexus. Nothing. It took another step forward, and Duncan pressed the trigger again.

-click-

Duncan looked down at his weapon with shock as the Womb slowly crouched down, then leaped forward with blinding speed and dug the talons of both its index fingers into Duncan's eye sockets. They ran down his face like tears made of jelly. He screamed so loud that his ears popped. So loud that he didn't even think the sound was coming from his own mouth, that it was someone else. It was only when a small trickle of his eye found its way into his own mouth that he came back to reality, though he wished he hadn't. The Womb drew back, then extended its arm right through Duncan's chest.

His heart fell to the ground on the other side of him, bouncing off the concrete from the propulsion of the blow.

The screaming stopped.

The Womb withdrew its arm from Duncan. It was coated from the shoulder down with dark redness.

The Womb turned, a wry smile on its face, searching out its next victim.

It snarled.

There, in the light of the doorway, Mandy Peterson lay in the arms of Randy Owchar. He had Ian's gun grasped in one hand, its barrel pointed against her chest. A taser shook in his other hand and he held it out toward the Womb, blue electricity coursing between its dual prongs and making the air smell like ozone. He held it out like a shield, as though he thought it would protect him.

"D-don't move!" he cautioned, stammering. "I mean it! I'll kill her!"

The Womb stood there, tilting its head to one side as Mandy watched it with sleepy but alert eyes, a smile somehow prying over her bludgeoned lips.

"You came..." she said weakly, blood coming out of her mouth.

"Yeah, well now I'll get to kill you both." Randy proclaimed proudly, gaining confidence with every word he convinced himself was true.

Slowly, the Black Womb crouched, tilting its head at Randy again.

"Bastard..." Randy whispered, tears flowing down his face. "This isn't the way it was supposed to go..."

"What?" the Womb said, its eyes melting from green to red. "You thought you were going to march into my school, kill people, kidnap and rape one of my friends, and then we were going to go outside and play jax?

"Grow up. Hand over the girl, before I get really mad again."

"No!" Randy yelled, putting first pressure on the trigger.

The Womb leaped, as fast as it could under Xander's control.

Randy fired.

BANG!

Mandy slumped to the floor, fresh blood soaking the wall.

"No!" Xander yelled in mid air, pummeling Randy and trying to wrestle the gun away. Randy brought the taser up fast and hit him in the right side. Electric fire spat out of it and shot through him.

The Womb sputtered, then died.

Even as the black liquid began to flow off of the naked Xander, he still tried to wrestle the gun away from the boy.

BANG!

BECOMING
CHAPTER TWENTY-ONE

Earlier that morning.

Mandy Peterson lay on the couch of Dr. Warren O'Toole, her hands folded in front of her, her eyes closed. She was asleep, or rather in a state of hypnosis, as the Counselor waved a golden pocket watch in front of her face.

"How do you feel, Mandy?" he asked her in a calm, steady voice, placing the watch on the table and picking up his pad and pencil.

"I'm a lot better today, actually." she smiled.

"Really, and why is that?"

"Last night I threw away all my old diaries and started a new one."

"Really? Why did you do that?"

"That was my old life. I didn't want to think about that anymore. I wanted to stop looking back and blaming myself and my mother and her boyfriends and my boyfriends... I just wanted to get on with my life, you know?"

Warren's lower lip quivered a moment, then he nodded, although she could not see him. He looked at her, at how beautiful she was, so sweet and innocent, healthily plump for a girl her age. The boys must love her.

"I do." he said finally, realizing that he hadn't verbally responded. "I do."

"I want to forget about them. I forgive them."

"You forgive them?" he said, dropping his pen.

"Yes, I do. I really do. That's why I had to throw away all the bad things I wrote about them all over the years. I want to start a new diary with good people in it. Like Xander, and they way he tries to make everybody okay, even when he's not. How he cares for me, though he doesn't have to. And Mike and Cathy, and how they love each other and how great that love is, even if they don't always see it. And Tommy... one of the only people to be so bad, and have something so bad happen to him... and then come out of it so good. So good.

"And Julie. I love her so much, I've never had a sister before.

"See? I want to write a new story, where nobody gets hurt and nobody cries. With people like my friends in it. And you, Dr. O'Toole."

Warren started to cry.

"I want to write something like that. I want that to be my life. And I can't wait to live it."

He wiped his tears long enough to say: "You can wake up now, Amanda."

Mandy awoke suddenly, her eyelids clicking softly as they snapped open. At first she wasn't quite sure where she was, looking up at an off-white stucco ceiling, her heart rate racing so much that she could hear it pounding in her ears.

"That was a good session." Warren said from where he sat perched on his chair across the room. He was still scribbling notes onto the sheet of paper attached to his clipboard, his hand going a mile a minute.

"It seems like I just laid down." she said groggily, sitting up and putting her hair back in a pony tail, pushing the hair away from her cute, plump face. Her sweater kept her warm on this chilly day, so big on her that it only stopped halfway between her hips and her knees. It made her look innocent and sweet, two words anyone that really knew her would probably not use to describe her.

"You always say that." he grinned, shoving his pocket watch into his breast pocket, his hand covered by a red and white handkerchief. "It's the truest sign of a good session."

"And you always say that." she pointed out, smiling at him just a little.

He smiled, but seemed distant. She wasn't sure, but she thought she caught the glimmer of tears in his eyes.

"So, when will you need to see me again?" she asked, stretching wide and then sighing happily.

"Hmm?" Warren hummed, lost in a stray thought. "Oh, yes. I'm sorry... um, let's say next week sometime. Contact me on Friday and we'll see when's a good time for you, okay?"

"Whatever." she chirped, then turned toward the door.

Warren watched her leave, then collapsed back into his chair, visibly exhausted.

"Oh, God..." he mumbled as reached behind his desk and pulled out a bottle of Jack Daniels and a short, wide glass. Throwing his clipboard into the nearest open cabinet, he poured himself a drink.

"Once more into the breach, my friends..." he murmured, downing the contents of the glass as fast as he could. "We few... we happy few."

BECOMING
CHAPTER TWENTY-TWO

Randy Owchar's hand slumped lifelessly to the floor, dropping the smoking gun as his last breath hissed from between his lips.

Xander, still dripping Womb-blood but not caring, rushed to Mandy's side. He propped her head up on his lap and he brushed the hair out of her broken face.

She tried to speak to him, but he shook his head.

"Shh..." he cautioned, hot tears streaming down his face as he held her close, her body... so cold. "Don't speak. It's gonna be okay. You're gonna be okay, I'm gonna get you help, love. Don't you -"

She raised a hand up to the side of his face and stroked it softly.

The last of the Womb's flesh dripped off of him.

"So," she whispered hoarsely. "You're the guy everybody's been talking about..."

Her hand fell from his face to the ground with an unceremonious thud, leaving only the blood that had been on her hand behind. Several long moments passed, as

Xander listened to her heart slow... then finally come to a stop.

His lower lip quivered as he reached up and closed her eyes for her, those beautiful, sparkling eyes that now seemed so dull and faded. Tears pitted against her cheeks, but she made no move to wipe them off. Slowly, he wrapped his arms around her and began rocking back and forth, cradling Mandy as the tears rushed from his eyes and nose.

He wanted to sing to her, that Irish song Sara used to sing to him, but his throat was too raked with tears, ravaged in a way nothing had ever been.

So he stayed there, rocking her back and forth, sobbing and convulsing. When finally he got the strength to speak, he screamed:

"BLACK WOMB LIVES!"

BECOMING
CLOSING

Genblade lived.

Genblade and Roulette had lived, both of them in jail now.

Somehow he found that one of the harder points to get past. Of all the people that had died in such a short amount of time, a person like Adam Genblade had survived. His spinal column injured, unable to speak or breathe on his own, possibly forever... but alive.

"Ashes, to ashes..." said Reverend Gallagher, as Mandy's casket was lowered into the ground, a few flakes of snow falling from the sky. "And dust, to dust..."

Mandy had always loved the snow, or so Xander had recalled her once saying. Now, she would never get to see it again.

"Nobody's here..." Cathy mumbled, looking around at the surprisingly small crowd gathered.

"Julie's still in the hospital." Xander said coldly, not turning away from the coffin as it landed in its hole with a dull thud. "Tommy wanted to stay with her, since her whole family was going to be here. Mike doesn't go to funerals anymore."

Cathy nodded, remembering her lover's stance on the dead.

"She was special." he said, mostly to himself.

Tears started to stream down Cathy's face. "You did everything you could."

Xander thought back, thought of the choice he'd made to go back and fight Genblade instead of searching for Mandy, who was right where he thought she'd be.

"Sure I did." he responded, trying to hide the sarcasm in his voice.

Circe was nowhere in sight. Xander had checked everywhere for Hale, but there wasn't even a trace of his scent. It was like he had never been there.

School would start up again soon, and everything would get back to normal.

Without her.

Once again, they were forced to leave someone behind and to press forward. To commit to continuing to live, if only to honor the memories of those who could not make such commitments.

Once again, good people had died when the bad continued to live.

"It should have been me." Xander said finally, drawing Cathy's attention.

"What?"

"It should have been me. I should have been faster, smarter... or just plain ignored O'Toole. I made every wrong choice that day."

"Xander..." she sighed, crying, unable to think of a

way to finish the sentence that would make him feel better.

"I have been asked by a shared friend of Mandy Peterson and I..." The Reverend continued, reaching down into his robe. "...to read to passage from the journal of Miss. Peterson."

Xander rose his head, eyes blank as he listened.

Gallagher opened the book, flipped a few pages ahead, then went back.

Tears started to flow down Xander's cheeks.

Though she wasn't quite sure why, when Cathy saw it, she cried.

Gallagher coughed.

"There is only one passage," he said, his lower lip shaking as he, too, started to cry. "It... It is dated the night before her death. It reads simply : 'I love my life. I can't wait to live it.'"

Cathy broke down crying, her tears washed away by the earth.

Gallagher stepped down, wiping his eyes in his sleeve as the rest of those gathered broke down as well.

Xander just stared down at the grave, as stone-faced as the headstone as his tears washed away his sins. He turned, looking up at Sara's grave on the hill, and listened.

"Hale said that I was becoming something." he said, to Sara as much as to Cathy, as he took her hand and lead her both away from the somber scene. "If that's true, then let it at least be something that I can stand to look at in the mirror."

PREVIEW

INNER CHILD

PREVIEW
INNER CHILD

"In the darkness it followed them, just enough light for them to see. It chased them through the brush and the woods, the tree limbs scraping past them, tearing at their limbs, cutting deep, deep, everything cut deep. The wind whistled through the branches as they ran past, singing the songs of their deaths, and it was beautiful.

"It was not an evil thing that pursued them, for its need to kill went far deeper than what we mere mortals define as right and wrong. It was simply a need to be, an urge to sate the growing hunger for flesh. It did not hate them, nor they it, because they knew that it was its instinct to give chase, as much as it was theirs to run.

"The ground beneath its feet stuck to it, keeping it moist and warm; a loud sucking sound accompanying every powerful stride as it broke the twigs that sliced at its prey, its eyes never batting for fear of being prodded. It thought only of the hunt, of the taste of victory.

"The moon overhead and the ground beneath, it chased as they were chased. It ran as they did run. And as it caught them, their flesh biding mercy to its claw, they became one under a common need, a common goal, and came to know and understand each other in the hour of their passing.

"The need to go on."

Alexander "Xander" Drew sat on the edge of his bed and stared down at the soft, carpeted floor of his bedroom. It was five-thirty in the morning and he had yet to shut his eyes, other than to blink when necessary.

He watched his hands, clasped loosely in front of him. They were shaking. They had been for the better part of an hour now, all of which he had spent looking at them and willing them not to shake. And yet, they refused to do so.

His palms were cold and sweaty, beads of moisture dripping off them down onto the floor. They were covered in scars and gaping wounds that only he could see, long since healed. In his mind's eye his wrists bled and the liquid dripping from them was a dark crimson, splashing down upon the carpet in great bursts and staining it forever. But like all things, it would heal in time. Everything here healed.

He was bare from the waist, covered in goosebumps from the harsh winter winds that made it in through his windowsill, and yet he was not cold. His body was covered in scars, too, but some of them were actually there. One was deep, still throbbing with pain every now and again, over his right side. Some that did not know him often asked if that was where his appendix had been taken out. In fact, it was where his life had been taken out, and exposed for all to see.

Other marks were invisible, like the one over his heart. He often wondered how many times a heart could be ripped out and yet still be there, still feel, still beat. Alone in the darkness, he often wished that it was gone.

His square jaw was set, his teeth clenched in determination. Every breath made his cheeks quiver and shake with frustration. His molars ground together, making a sound that even he found unpleasant, his ear lobes twitching around uncut swatches of auburn hair wet and sticky with sweat.

His eyes twitched, their blue irises fixated on his quaking

fingertips. Veins had begun to form in their sclera from stress and lack of sleep. His brow furrowed, eyebrows slanting as he tried even harder to stop, and they only seemed to convulse more.

His mouth was dry and tasted of copper. He kept clacking his tongue against the roof of it and expecting to find blood, but there was none. Yet the taste remained, just like the scars.

His long nose was red from the chill, a stray drop of mucus falling from it every now and again onto his checkered flannel pajama bottoms. He responded only with an exaggerated sniff, not wanting to move away or do anything that would move his disobedient hands from view.

"Guh," he gasped finally, realizing that he had been holding his breath, his chest heaving as oxygen burned at his aching lungs.

The gaping maw of a cut on his left wrist poured out blood just as water poured from a faucet, never ending, never bringing him peace. No, never peace.

He reached down slowly with his right hand, keeping one eye trained on them on the off chance that it stopped shaking. It had not stopped shaking all the while he was in the shower, no matter how hot he had made the water. It had not stopped long enough for him to suffer down his mother's meat loaf, the fork almost falling from his trembling hands.

But maybe it would stop shaking now.

He reached under his bed and pushed aside the box of old monster comics and an unopened set of computer disks, his hand finally finding a wooden box pushed deep beneath the mattress. He clasped it firmly and pulled it out.

Across from him, against the far wall of his room, his computer monitor stared blankly at him. He had not turned it on in days, and now it stared back at him in the dark like a never-ending void. Like the abyss.

He placed the box upon his lap and ran his fingers along its smooth surface, his thumbnail catching on the frayed and splintered corners. He looked at it silently for a long moment, then lifted the cover and revealed its red velvet interior.

The light that reflected off of its contents illuminated his face, gleaming off of his eyes. It was a knife, roughly a foot long from the tip of its blade to the end of its handle. A dagger then, to be precise. It was inside a metal sheath decorated by a carving of a long line of fire, which made light sparkle and dance off of it. The flames came from the mouth of the dragon that occupied the handle, its mouth gaping open toward the blade, tail swirling down to the bottom.

His eyes darted in their sockets toward the door, making sure that it was shut tight and locked.

He picked up the blade and pressed the locking mechanism near his thumb, shifting it to the right with ease and detaching the dagger from its hilt. He placed the case back into the box gently, and then closed the lid.

On the blade itself there were markings on it that looked Cantonese but weren't, weren't anything that he could find online or in the books at school. There was blood on it already, but it was not his. No, much worse. It was the blood of someone he could not save, and it could be seen by more than just him... but he saw it everywhere, especially on his hands.

Frowning at his reflection in the steel, he turned back toward his disobedient left hand, wrist facing up.

It was already bleeding in his mind's eye.

He pressed the tip of the dagger to where he saw the cut begin in his head, slowly applying pressure until it punctured through the flesh, a small pool of blood pushing up from around it. Slowly, methodically, he traced the cut he saw with his cold steel pen, sketching out what he knew in his damned heart was right.

The blood came now in a splash as he dropped the dagger to the floor. The sound woke him, made him know that this was real and not just another illusion that his mind had created for him. This was happening, and he was strangely glad.

Pain ruptured from the open wound as the blood squirted out. Slowly, painfully, his vein filled eyes rolled back into his head. All of the colour drained from his face until he was as white as the paper that was scattered around his floor.

He clenched his teeth even harder as his body threw itself backward, slamming his head against the sloping wall of his room and falling onto his bed where his hands finally stopped shaking. The flow of redness slowed to a weak dribble, and his lungs released their final breath.

There was nothing but silence for three long minutes, as the space heater in the corner struggled to kick in and fight against the raging storm outside.

Deep inside his chest, his heart let out a final, pitiful hum as it stopped beating.

Something stirred to life in his abdomen and began to beat the second that his heart failed to do so.

His left hand twitched, ever so slightly. Then again.

It twitched and blood started to come out of it. This time his blood was a deep, thick black, and instead of flowing down and staining his dark sheets like the rest it began to flow upward against the pull of gravity, toward his fingers.

Inching along like a million ebony earthworms, growing with every pump of Xander's black heart, it slowly made its way upward.

It trickled slowly, swirling around his pinky finger and enveloping it in darkness before moving on to the ring finger, picking up speed and confidence with every square centimetre of flesh that it took as its own.

All at once, the pinky started to twitch and bend, coming back to life and exercising its right to move. Slowly, a point poked its way out of its tip and grew into a long slender talon. The black bone gleamed against the dim light in the room the same way that the blade had, reflecting the pictures in their frames that lined his computer desk. Pictures of *her*. Pictures of them. Pictures of those that for all his effort he could not save. And the latest...

The blackness took his entire hand, the bones in his knuckles and the joints of his fingers snapping and crackling as they snapped in two and then healed themselves simultaneously, creating new tissue and marrow to fill the gaps, making his fingers longer. The darkness met with the cut where it had originally started, and for a moment looked like a thin leather glove covering his hand before the trail continued down his arm, swirling about and picking up steam.

His elbow cracked, bending in the opposite direction, then circled around until it was upright again, twisting and ruining flesh before it was taken over by the darkness, making it look smooth again.

The ooze on his hand began to dry, crackling like the ground over the desert as the moisture left it, turning it into small, square scales.

Xander's eyes snapped open with a barely audible click, his pupils rolling back into position, only now they were larger and darker. The blue irises had disappeared, taken over completely by the pupils that now refused to reflect light of any kind. The red veins in his eyes were gone, instead becoming the same deep black that was overcoming the rest of him.

"Guh," he managed to say again. He was trying to speak, to scream out the pain and fright that came over him along with the blood. Instead blackness erupted from his lips and vomited out onto his chest and stomach, joining with the first trail and hastening its decent downward.

All of the fat remaining on his abdomen was devoured, absorbed by the beast as it pressed on, seeming to only grow in hunger with every bite it took from his flesh. His rib cage (short one rib for months now) expanded outward as the cartilage grew, as if it were going to break free of the new flesh. The ooze piled into the puddle that had been Xander's stomach, churning about and forming muscles before working its way downward.

The blackness that Xander had spewed onto his chest dug into his flesh until it reached the breast plate, wedging itself into it and spreading it apart, opening his chest as wide as possible while rising, turning the fat and existing skin tissue into brawn and sinew.

It flowed down his legs, eliminating fat there as well, replacing it with thin, sleek tone. There was a gut-wrenching crack as his kneecap shattered and his bones broke, his entire leg shaking as it bent back the other way, like a horses hind legs, then back again, moving at will like the hinge of a door caught in the wind.

His ankles disappeared, the substance from which went toward expanding the mass of each respective foot, each gaining length and becoming more pointed, perfect for jumping and leaping long distances now.

His head thrashed back and forth as the blackness traveled up his neck, flattening his hair to his skull until it looked as though there was none, circling around his head to come at his face from all sides.

The organ deep inside his right side trashed and convulsed violently, pumping as hard as it could. It wanted to win, wanted to be free more than anything else.

His eyes darted back and forth as the blackness swallowed his face whole like a giant, gaping mouth until there was nothing but the white of his eyes left, and in a moment, his pupils finished expanding, relieving him of those as well.

He stopped twitching and all was silent and still and dead. There was a short snap as his nose broke, sinking down to form a curve all the way down his face. The ooze on his head dried into the bald shadow-figure it had so many times before.

Slowly, three curved red lines drew themselves on his face, as if someone were standing over him with a pencil. The top two diagonal lines opened, revealing themselves to be red, pupil-less eyes. They stared blankly and emotionlessly into the void before it, glowing and turning upward like a cat's.

The third line opened from the bottom down, showing off two long rows of serrated yellow teeth that went further back than any human set ever did. A pinkish tongue whipped around and about, saliva dripping from it.

When it spoke its words were course and rough, its throat

ripped raw from blood and stomach acid.

"Black Womb lives."

It growled, bending its knees and standing up. It looked down with those large, opaque eyes at the pool of blood on the floor, sniffing twice. It closed its mouth, and when it did it seemed to disappear into a thin straight line across its face. It turned, first with its head and long neck and then with the rest of its body, toward the window. It still whistled cold air despite the noisy protests of the space heater. It walked to the window, clutched its release with its clawed fingers, and pushed upward. Snow billowed in, the entire blizzard seeming to want to enter the room all at once.

Feeling the wind but not the cold, the creature reached out the window, dug its claws into the side of the house and scaled its way down. The window slammed shut behind it.

Carefully, it leapt to the ground and walked into the thick Maine forest behind the house. Within seconds, it had sprinted across the yard and the yard next door and was hidden by the darkness of the brush, where nothing would see it even if it were directly in front of them.

ENGEN TIMELINE

With over twenty novels spread over three different series by many different authors, the Engen Universe of titles is growing every day and into genres we couldn't have imagined! From the original ten book *Coral Beach Casefiles* thriller series, its crime novel sequel series *Xander Drew*, our flagship adventure title *Infinity*, or single-novels like *Jacobi Street* or *light|dark*, there's something in the Engen Universe for everyone with more books by more authors on the way soon!

...But how do the events relate to one another, chronologically? While some astute readers have guessed at the potential timeline (some accurately, some not), we're going to finally set the question of the Engen Timeline to rest.

Turn the page for an up-to-date guide of the ever-widening world of Engen, featuring the works of Ellen Curtis, Andrea Hackett, Sarah Thompson, Jay Paulin, and Matthew LeDrew!

In the 10 Years Prior Black September

"Reptilia" by Matthew LeDrew
published in *light I dark* & *Collected Short Fiction*
"Reptilian" by Paul Carberry
published in *Undead Rebirth*.
Danger descends on a small secluded town in the form of a deadly virus with fantastic and terrible side-effects. Can a small group of doctors escape alive?

Compendium by Ellen Curtis
Three short stories forming the basis for the Engen Universe's ties to suspense, genetic engeneering, and the supernatural. Features the stories "The Tourniquet Revival," "Falling into Fire" and "At Midnight, the Dawn."

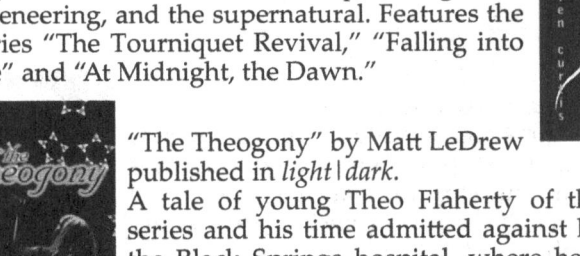

"The Theogony" by Matt LeDrew
published in *light I dark*.
A tale of young Theo Flaherty of the *Infinity* series and his time admitted against his will to the Black Springs hospital, where he learns to paint, and seeks out his father.

Black September

"Revving Engen" by Matthew LeDrew
published in *light I dark*.
A direct lead-in to both *Infinity* and *Black Womb*, Tasha travels to Coral Beach, Maine on a hot tip about a recently discovered young man with incredible abilities.

Infinity by Ellen Curtis & Matthew LeDrew
Faced with a destiny he's uncertain of, the enigmatic Victor must bring together four unique people with very special abilities... or face the tasks ahead alone. Guaranteed to excite!

Black Womb by Matthew LeDrew
Fifteen years ago, something happened in Coral Beach, Maine that resulted in the present death of a seventeen-year-old boy. Now four high-school students must try to solve the mystery… before the killer picks them off.

Jacobi Street by Matthew LeDrew
When a mysterious painting shows up at an art gallery he works at, Bob must work with Eddie and Sloan to track down its sinister origins and convince the people living on Jacobi Street of them, before its too late!

Transformations in Pain by Matthew LeDrew
When two girls are assaulted, the residents of Coral Beach must put their shared tragedies behind them and stop the man responsible, as well as unlock the secrets behind the true nature of the Womb…

Variety Show by Ali House
Local performer Wendy is introduced to the drama and mystique of The Quaint Little Theatre of Jacobi Street. But backstabbing aren't the only dangers at play in this venue...

Smoke and Mirrors by Matthew LeDrew
The approaching trial of Genblade brings closure to the people of Coral Beach, until people start showing up dead in the same manner they did when he was at large.

"The Inevitable" by Ali House
published in *The Lightbulb Forest*
A young woman must contend with the emergence of a frightening new power alongside the emotional high of a first date.

The Tourniquet Reprisal by Curtis & LeDrew
A man lives in Atlanta, Georgia that people don't talk about, but everyone knows he's there. He arrived a year ago and turned a gaggle of uneducated youth into something new, something to fear.

Roulette by Matthew LeDrew
As the teen suicide rate in Coral Beach starts to climb astronomically fast, Xander travels to Los Angeles to fight his most terrifying adversary yet… and learns that the only thing worse than looking for release… is finding it.

Year One: November

Exodus of Angels by Curtis & LeDrew
Victor's enigmatic past is illuminated when Jaycee accompanies him to visit a new friend in the paliative care ward of the Black Springs hospital, where Theo also happens to be searching for a cure for Leigh.

The Irony of Glass by Matthew Daniels
published in *Undead Rebirth* and *Interstitches.*
Abby and Chad track down a man with the ability to project his emotional state to a remote town, and struggle to escape.

Ghosts of the Past by Matthew LeDrew
Coral Beach faces its most awesome threat when
one of Engen's past mistakes is unleashed upon
the unsuspecting populous. Friends and enemies
unite to fight a common enemy... but will even
that be enough?

Touch Your Nose by Matt LeDrew
Simon Monk must infiltrate the San Fransico
branch of Shane Industries, a massive company
with deep ties to the Engen Universe. Where do
his true loyalties lie? And can he get out without
causing harm?

Ignorance is Bliss by Matthew LeDrew
After being set through the ringer one too many
times, Xander decides that his life with Julie
needs a little more attention... which is bad news
because a new villain has come to town with his
sights set on Adam Genblade.

"Gristle While You Work" by Jay Paulin &
"Scarlett" by Andrea Hackett
published in *light | dark*.

"A Night to Forget" by Kelly Rose &
"New Employment" by Sam Bauer
published in *Undead Rebirth*.

Becoming by Matthew LeDrew
For months Xander Drew has been doing his
level best to keep the streets of Coral Beach clean,
which means it's time for the forces of darkness
to strike back... all at once.

Inner Child by Matthew LeDrew
Julie is hospitalized with life-threatening wounds to both body and soul. But the real threat comes from the hospital walls themselves, as a demonic presence makes itself known to Xander and his friends.

"Comfortably Numb" by Ellen Curtis
published in *Undead Rebirth.*
Xander and Cathy spend an evening hunting the remnants of Coral Beach's gangs when Xander begins to lose control of the Black Womb, threatening their secret.

End of Year One

Gang War by Matthew LeDrew
The Tees, a homicidal gang of evil men, has finally been taken down by Xander Drew. But his victory is short lived, as retired Tees are mysteriously killed. With a town of suspects, anyone can be the culprit... including one of their own.

Chains by Matthew LeDrew
Sociopath Derek Smith has been freed from prison and is praying on the weak; and none are weaker than August Styles: a pregnant girl with Down Syndrome who has run away from home.

"Omega" by Ellen Curtis
published in *light | dark.*
A sinister division of Engen begins a series of experiments on pregnant women in a fashion eerily similar to those that created the original Black Womb project.

The Long Road by Matthew LeDrew
Xander meets the American people — and realizes that the world is harsh and wicked, but can also be soft and gentle, even loving. Xander Drew comes of age on the road, and sets his new direction.

Year Two

Cinders by Matthew LeDrew
Detective Horton enters a violent and dangerous world he didn't know existed beneath the veneer of order and structure that he has based his entire deductive method around.

Sinister Intent by Matthew LeDrew
One of the killers Detective Horton could not catch has resurfaced: a serial killer who flaunts his sinister intent in front of the Los Angeles Police Department, making it so that no one is safe.

Faith by Matthew LeDrew
Xander's mysterious and troublesome past returns to haunt him on the streets of Los Angeles; a place where even more people can get caught in the crossfire of the games of death and deceit that makes up his life.

Flickers in the Night by Matthew LeDrew
Lisa Rowdan is hunted by her haunting -- and powerful -- ex-boyfriend Ryan through a lonely city street. Can she escape him?

One of over twenty great sprine-tingling short stories!

Garden of the 8th Circle by Curtis & LeDrew
Victor brings Chad, Abby, and Alice into a dangerous conflict a decade in the making, fighting an out of control cult for the fate of a young soul. Meanwhile, Theo investigates a mysterious event in Los Angeles.

Family Values by Matthew LeDrew
Xander and his new friends Crowley, Lisa, and Tim investigate a series of kidnappings and murders that stretch back decades, all of which have the same similar twist: victims being found after years of being missing.

The Rats of Refraction by Curtis & LeDrew
When Abby and Alice's secret lives are discovered, they must defend their home and way of life with everything they have against the forces of Circe, a shadow agency that will stop at nothing to abduct people with supernatural abilities.

Fate's Shadow by Matthew LeDrew
When one of Xander's old cases comes up for trial, Megan Greene returns with it. The former friends are led into conflict regarding her client's innocence. However, they put their difference aside when they both become targets of the vigilante known as Shiro Gilbert.

First Aid by Matthew LeDrew
Xander takes his feud with mob boss Stephen Fields to the streets, and his attracts the attention of the *Infinity* team. Before the arrive, he'll have pushed the mob boss into an all out gang war, the likes of which the city will never recover from.

As Loved Our Fathers by Matthew LeDrew

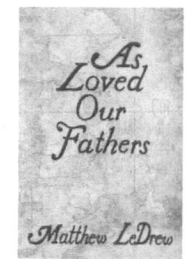

Jona's plans come into view as he travels to the island of Newfoundland in search of a mystical item: the Holy Grail.

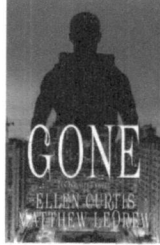

Gone by Curtis & LeDrew
Chad's sister has gone missing, resulting in him upending heaven and hell to get her back. His quest embroils him back into the dangerous world he'd hoped to escape, and unlocks the terrible secrets Jona has been investigating.

Moments by Matthew LeDrew
The Shane murders have been happening for months, dogging Xander at every turn. They've been happening for longer than even he knows, stretching back to the Black September. He's taken down Fields. He's taken down Murdock. Now the stage is set for this part of the story to also end.

Exposure by Erin Vance
Joshua Deering just wanted was to pass his final photography project. But that's not what happened. But hindsight is 20/20, and now creepy cemetery guy Adrian, Josh, and Josh's two friends are being stalked by nameless, violent strangers.

"The Port 13 Motel" by Erin Vance &
"Living Light" by Sam Bauer
published in *Undead Rebirth*.

The unlikely return of both Kemp and a cannibalistic serial killer to the Engen Universe.

The Future

"Remers" by Sarah Thompson
published in *light | dark*.
In the not-too-distant future of the Engen
Universe, young athletes are the targets of a
scouting program to create the next stage of
super soldier with cybernetic enhancements.

Timeline I - V by Matthew LeDrew
published in *Undead Rebirth & Collected Shorts*
Faced with the death of his wife, Mikhail
breaks the laws of time and space to find a
way to save her, only to discover that her fate
was sealed in the distant past...

ABOUT THE AUTHOR

Matthew LeDrew holds an Honours Degree in English from the Memorial University of Newfoundland with a minor in Anthropology, and studied Journalism at College of the North Atlantic in Stephenville, Newfoundland. He was honoured to be a jury member of the 2018 NLBA awards.

He has written twenty novels for Engen Books: the ten book *Coral Beach Casefiles* series, *The Long Road, Cinders, Sinister Intent, Faith, Family Values, Jacobi Street, Touch Your Nose, Infinity, The Tourniquet Reprisal, and Exodus of Angels* the latter three of which with co-author Ellen Curtis.

He lives in St. Johns, Newfoundland.

www.ingramcontent.com/pod-product-compliance
Lightning Source LLC
Chambersburg PA
CBHW011435240626

47153CB00011B/3003